KU-353-815

ENDING IN TEARS

12-year-old Sally Luckham, the victim of a failed abduction attempt, cannot give detectives any clues, except that her attacker was a woman with shining black hair. Another young girl has recently gone missing, and psychologist Anna McColl is brought in to coax Sally's memory. Anna finds herself drawn to the lonely young girl, and learns that Sally's father Tom had died six months previously, in a suspicious fall. Tom was loved and admired by everyone, so who would want to murder him? As Anna begins her own investigation, she finds she is being shadowed by a woman with very dark, shiny hair...

ENDING IN
TEARS

by

Penny Kline

Magna Large Print Books
Long Preston, North Yorkshire,
England.

British Library Cataloguing in Publication Data.

Kline, Penny
   Ending in tears.

   A catalogue record for this book is
   available from the British Library

   ISBN 0-7505-1172-9

First published in Great Britain by Macmillan, an imprint of
Macmillan Publishers Ltd., 1997

Copyright © 1997 by Penny Kline

Cover illustration © Bruno Brogna

The right of Penny Kline to be identified as the author of
this work has been asserted by her in accordance with the
Copyright, Designs and Patents Act, 1988

Published in Large Print 1997 by arrangement with Macmillan
General Books.

All rights reserved. No part of this publication may be
reproduced, stored in a retrieval system, or transmitted in any
form or by any means, electronic, mechanical, photocopying,
recording or otherwise, without the prior permission of the
Copyright owner.

Magna Large Print is an imprint of
Library Magna Books Ltd.
Printed and bound in Great Britain by
T.J. International Ltd., Cornwall, PL28 8RW.

Chapter One

Sally, Sally, pride of our alley. Singing that was more like shouting, like a football crowd, except there were only four of them. Josie, Cherie, Tara—and Abigail. They had been waiting for her by the downstairs toilets and if she had tried to squeeze past they would have blocked her way, then let her by and listened outside the cubicle. Josie giggling. Abigail whispering. *Her hair! Still, I suppose it looks a bit better since she took my advice and tied it back.* Tara laughing, always laughing. *Well, it couldn't look worse.*

Sometimes, lying in bed, she thought she could hear Abigail, in the hall, or out in the garden. *Abigail, Abigail Knox. I'm a friend of Sally's, from school. Well, not a friend exactly. She's in my class.* But that was impossible. Abigail would never call round at the house...

She was bursting, but she could last till she got home. She had to. Feeling behind her head, as she walked, half ran, she pushed up the blue rubber band, dragging the hairs on the back of her neck until her eyes filled with tears. The pain helped, so did the feel of the Crunchie bar in her blazer pocket. She took it out, tearing the paper at one end, glancing over her shoulder at the car that was following her. But not really. It was just a game she played. The driver was a woman, with dark glasses and glossy brown hair, tied back loosely so that some of it still covered her ears, and Sally could see she was a stranger to the area, crawling along, slowing down to check the name of each side street. There was no one else about. Perhaps the woman would stop and ask her the way. She was good at giving directions. Sometimes she rehearsed them in her head. *The quickest way to Whiteladies Road? Yes, no problem. Turn right at the end there, then first left, then straight on...*

''Scuse me, love, I'm looking for Lincoln Road.'

'Oh.' The driver had her head turned to the left, studying a map. Her voice didn't match Sally's image of her, and the car engine was terribly noisy, so she might have heard wrong. 'You don't mean Linden Road?'

'Could be.' The woman climbed out of the car, still with her head turned away, and held out the curled-up map.

'We're here,' said Sally, pointing with the long nail on her index finger that Abigail had said was common. 'Only, if you want Linden Road you'll have to...'

She never finished the sentence. The woman grabbed her from behind, squeezing her so tight that when she tried to call out there was no air in her lungs. Struggling to break free, she caught her hand on the sharp edge of the car door and suddenly the terror that had made her so weak and helpless gave way to fury. Opening her mouth wide, she twisted her head, like an angry dog, and sank her teeth into the thin cotton of the woman's shirt. For a split second the grip loosened. Sally ducked under the woman's arm, then forced her legs to start running. The woman would catch up with her, she knew she would, but there was just a chance another car might come round the corner. Would the driver help, or would he think she was playing some kind of game? Unable to stop herself looking back, she was just in time to see the woman jump into her car and slam the door. A moment later it mounted the pavement, almost hitting a tree, then raced towards her, braked sharply, and spun round, facing in the opposite direction. As it turned, Sally caught sight of the driver's face—the first time she had seen it properly—and let out a small cry of disbelief. It couldn't have been. She must have made a mistake.

Then, with tyres squealing, the car shot off in the direction of Shirehampton, swerving from side to side until it finally disappeared round a bend in the road. Still fighting for breath, Sally leaned against a tree, felt her body go limp, and watched dispassionately as the warm liquid trickled down the inside of her legs and soaked into her socks.

Chapter Two

If Superintendent Fry had called me in sooner it might have spared Sally Luckham a lot of grief. At the very least he could have made sure it was Sergeant Whittle who talked to her, not the new Inspector, DCI Ritsema who had the misfortune to believe he was 'good with children' and seemed to have treated the twelve-year-old as if she were about two and a half, then switched tactics and bullied her into silence. Lesley Stafford had given me a blow-by-blow account of the first interview. She had done her best to intervene but as a recent recruit to the CID, and a woman at that, her opinion had counted for less than nothing as far as DCI Ritsema was concerned.

In the minds of the local CID there was a definite possibility that Sally Luckham's attempted abduction had been carried out by the same person who had been responsible for a far more serious incident less than a month ago. Another schoolgirl had witnessed one of her classmates, a girl called Geena Robson, being pulled into a car by a woman driving down Cotham Hill. Since then, the girl's mother—her father was living with another woman—had received a couple of silent phone calls, but nothing had been seen of the fourteen-year-old victim. Friends, relatives and the girl's teachers had all been interviewed, then interviewed again. Suspected sightings in various parts of the country had been followed up, but the police still had no real leads—until the attempt to snatch the Luckham girl. My job was to calm her down, then help her remember more details about the car and its driver. So far she had been unable to provide the police with any information, apart from the fact that the driver had been a woman, with 'dark glasses and shiny brown hair'. Arriving home in tears, she had blurted out what had happened to the only person around at the time—the cleaning lady—then begged her not to report the incident. Fortunately the woman had picked up a phone and dialled 999.

The Luckham house was on the far side of the Downs, not a part of Bristol I visited very often, although I knew enough about the area to be aware that Sally Luckham could hardly be described as coming from an underprivileged home background, at least in economic terms. According to Howard Fry she attended a private school, about a mile and a half from where she lived, and it was while she was walking home, around midday, that the attempted abduction had taken place. It was the last day of the summer term, which accounted for the early release of the pupils. Normally she would have been walking along that particular road at nearer four-thirty, so either the abductor knew she would be leaving before lunch, or she had followed her from the school, or—and this seemed the most likely explanation—Sally was a random victim who just happened to be in the wrong place at the wrong time.

I kept thinking the abductor was a man, then remembering it was a woman. Why would a woman want to do such a thing, although it had been known before. A kidnapping? But in the case of Geena Robson there had been no ransom note. A woman procuring a child for her boyfriend? For some time the CID had been following up reports of two women who called round at people's houses saying they had come to make checks on babies and young children, then drove away pretty sharpish when asked to prove their identity.

Geena Robson's abductor had been a tall woman, with glasses and her hair in a ponytail. Sally had seemed uncertain about the height and build of her 'abductor', but in any case, neither description bore any resemblance to either of the bogus health visitors. For reasons Howard Fry had not thought fit to explain, the police seemed convinced that Geena Robson had been murdered, and DCI Ritsema was certain Sally Luckham, if she would only calm down and start thinking straight, could lead them to the killer.

Berry Drive, leading off Finefield Gardens, consisted of three large, detached houses overlooking the Avon Gorge. Not that the Gorge itself could be seen from the road, but Leigh Woods, on the other side, was just visible between the trees. The Larches was flanked on either side by Clifton Lodge and Westwinds. None of the houses was particularly old or particularly new. Each had a small garden at the front and a much larger one at the back.

I parked outside Westwinds—mine was the only car in the road—and flicked through the notes Howard Fry had provided, refreshing my memory about the family set-up: *Sally Luckham, aged twelve and a half, living with her widowed mother, Erica, and her eighteen-year-old brother, James.* Then the name of her school, together with the time of day, and the name of the road where the attempted abduction had taken place. Erica Luckham had no job, neither did James, although he had left school the previous Christmas.

In contrast to Whiteladies Road, where the traffic had held me up for ages, Berry Drive was amazingly quiet. Birds twittered, insects buzzed, someone in a garden called to a child to come indoors and put on some shoes. The sun had burned away the mist that had covered most of Bristol first thing, and now, at half past eleven, it could almost be described as a glorious summer's day. It was good to be out of the office. For the first time in several weeks I felt keyed up, full of energy. Maybe I needed a new job, one that kept me on the move. Maybe I just needed a change.

The Larches looked as if it had been built in the 1930s. Its white rendering and green pantiled roof must once have seemed the last word in modernity, and it was still an imposing place, if only because of its size, although, as far as I could see, the trees were all silver birch, with not a larch in sight. Beyond a half-open gate, with an ancient notice banning the entry of hawkers and traders, a short path, with rough grass on both sides, led up to a green front door that could have done with a coat of paint. The garage, a pebble-dashed building with a corrugated iron roof, was detached and had its own driveway, parallel with the path but outside the actual garden.

I had no idea what to expect but it was important to get off to a good start. Howard had phoned Mrs Luckham the previous evening to explain who I was, but when I asked him how she had taken the news that a psychologist was calling round to interview her daughter, he had adopted his usual non-committal air. *To tell you the truth, Anna, she didn't seem that interested. Strange woman, but I daresay she's still grieving for her husband, only stick to Sally, don't try and combine your visit with a spot of bereavement counselling...*

I rang the bell, but there was no response. No sounds inside the house, no voices calling to one another. After waiting thirty

14

seconds, I tried again and this time the door was pulled open at once by a thin woman with frizzy grey hair, a pink overall, and a look of mild exasperation on her face.

'I've come to see Mrs Luckham.'

'She's indisposed.' The woman had small, cold eyes, and appeared to have decided I was one of the forbidden hawkers.

'Dr McColl,' I said, irritated by the way she was looking me up and down. 'I have an appointment to see Sally, but I think I should talk to her mother first.'

'I told you, she's indisposed.' Her hands had been pushed into her overall pockets, but the glare had been replaced by something more like curiosity. 'Come inside, then. I'll see if I can find James.'

She disappeared into the house and I heard her opening and closing doors. A dog barked in the distance and I thought I could hear someone crying, but it could have been a small child playing. Several minutes later the woman returned.

'You're the psychologist, then,' she said crossly. 'Why didn't you say? Sally's in the drawing-room. Mrs Luckham says it's all right for you to talk to her now.' She pointed to a half-open door, then switched on an electric polisher, shouting above the noise, 'I'll bring some coffee when I've finished this lot.'

'Thanks.' I pushed open the door and found myself in a room that, at first sight, seemed large enough to contain the whole of my flat. In spite of the sunlight on the parquet floor, and the vivid brightness of the lawn beyond the patio doors, it felt chilly. The sofas and chairs had been upholstered in an unattractive sludge colour, and the five or six rugs, that had been scattered about the floor, were all in various hues of beige or cream. The wall lights had been switched on—their shades were parchment-coloured with silky fringes, and the bulb-holders had blobs of imitation wax running down their sides—but several had bulbs missing. A girl was sitting in one of the large armchairs at the far end of the room with her arms folded across her chest and her pale, freckled face as expressionless as she could make it. She was watching me, but pretending she had no idea I had entered the room.

'Sally?' I moved towards her, then sat on the arm of a sofa. 'My name's Dr McColl. Anna. I think you knew I was coming to see you.'

She stood up, then sat down again. She was dressed in green denim shorts that came to just below her knees, and a dark blue sweatshirt with a panda on the front. Her hair had been dragged back from her face and was kept in place with a blue rubber band that had been knotted several times. The skin close to her hair line was even paler than the rest of her face.

'The cleaner said your mother's not very well.'

Sally's shoulders twitched. 'She's all right.'

'Is your brother at home?'

'He's still in bed.'

'Yes, I see. Anyway, this won't take long, I hope. How've you been feeling? That was a horrible thing that happened to you. It must have been very frightening.'

A surprised expression was quickly turned into a frown. 'I wasn't hurt.'

'No, I know that. Even so...' I broke off, suddenly uneasy about conducting the conversation without Mrs Luckham being present. In a way, it made things easier, but it didn't seem fair on Sally. 'Listen, would you rather I came back when your mother's feeling better?'

'No!' She shook her head vigorously,

grasping her knees with both hands. 'I mean, I don't mind, it wouldn't make any difference.'

'All right, if you're sure, but if you change your mind, let me know. Right, well I think the best thing is if you start from the beginning, describe exactly what happened last Friday.'

'Didn't they tell you?' She had a nervous habit that made her twitch her nose repeatedly.

'Yes, but I'd prefer to hear it from you. When something unexpected happens none of us are very good at remembering exactly what we saw, but sometimes a day or two later small details gradually start to come back.'

She was picking at a small scab on her shin. Suddenly her head came up and she opened her mouth as if she was going to speak, then closed it again. I looked round the room, searching for a photo that might tell me something about the rest of the family. There were several paintings on the wall, including one of a field of sunflowers, but no photographs and very few ornaments. Perhaps it was a room they hardly ever used. The cleaner had found Sally in the garden, opened the patio door to let her into the house, told her where to sit, then returned to me, via the kitchen.

Sally was staring at me, but as soon as our eyes made contact she returned to picking at the scab.

'You were on your way home from school,' I said encouragingly. 'Where exactly is the school? Is it that one you pass on the way to——'

'I've tried to remember, honestly I have.' Her body was tense with anxiety. 'I just can't.'

'All right, don't worry. I'm not sure what happened when Inspector Ritsema talked to you, but I'm certainly not here to put you under any pressure. Just take your time, start from when you first came out of school at the end of the morning.'

'School?' Now she was winding a few hairs round her little finger. 'I'd walked quite a long way before...'

'Yes, I know, but it's possible whoever was in the car had been following you for some time.' As soon as the remark was out I regretted it. Poor kid, it was bad enough being the intended victim of a random abduction, now I was suggesting she might have been specially selected.

19

'I'd have seen the car before,' she said. 'I mean, if it was waiting outside school.'

'Yes, I'm sure you would.' I wanted to ask her how she had managed to struggle free. A slightly built twelve-year-old would have stood little chance against a fully grown woman, even allowing for the fact that she claimed to have bitten the woman's arm.

'Will I be hypnotized?' she asked, pulling her legs up under her and wriggling into a more comfortable position on the chair. 'James said I'd have to lie on the sofa and you'd swing a watch on a chain above my head. Then they make you say whatever they want and you're powerless to resist.'

'Nothing like that,' I said, smiling, and receiving a flicker of a smile in return. 'Don't make a huge effort to remember. Just try to relax, think about walking up the road, before it happened, as if it was an ordinary day.'

Whatever she had been asked before I was determined to allow her to describe things in her own way. Mountains of research into what's known as 'reconstructive memory' had demonstrated pretty conclusively how witnesses gather 'information' from leading questions and incorporate it

20

into their 'memory' of an event. In one instance, hundreds of people were asked to say whether the broken glass from a road accident had been in front of the car or to one side; only a handful had reported accurately that there had been no broken glass.

Upstairs, a vacuum cleaner had been switched on. So much for the promised coffee. Above the racket I thought I could hear someone shouting.

Sally was screwing up her face, opening and closing her mouth, biting her lip.

'What about the car,' I said. 'Was it a dark colour or a light one?'

'That's what everyone keeps asking, only I'm not interested in cars. I don't know any of the makes.' She was breathing hard. 'It could have been grey. It was just a car. Everyone expects me to remember, but I'm not good at that kind of thing, not like some people are. You can ask anybody.'

I waited until she calmed down a little, then tried again. 'How long had the car been following you before it drew level?'

'I'm not sure.' She stifled a yawn. If anyone needed a lie in...but she seemed to be the only member of the family who was up and about. 'They think it was like

21

that other girl, don't they, only I'm sure it wasn't.'

'No, I expect you're right. But what makes you think...'

She made a kind of gulping noise. 'I just know. I suppose it could've been the same person, but it's usually men who kill you, isn't it? I mean, I can see why the police want to find out as much as possible, and I know you're trying to help me, and if I could remember any more I'd tell you, of course I would.'

She was afraid, there was no doubt of that, but there was something else. She had started to choose her words carefully, as if she had been through them in her mind before I arrived and was trying to stick to a well-rehearsed script.

'James was going to be a scientist,' she said suddenly. 'Scientists have to write down exactly what they see, only when we do experiments at school they usually go wrong.'

'Yes, I know what you mean.' Memories of litmus paper that should have turned pink but didn't. Writing it up anyway, getting a tick if you reported the 'right' result, learning what was required. 'What kind of a scientist does your brother want to be?'

'Oh, he's not going to be one now. He dropped out last Christmas. He was doing his A levels. He's much cleverer than me, but he got fed up.'

The door opened and the woman in the pink overall backed into the room, carrying a tray. 'Not interrupting anything, am I?'

Sally sprang to her feet. 'Is Mummy still in bed?'

The woman nodded, chewing whatever was in her mouth, then swallowing it and running her tongue round her lips. 'Be down soon, pet.' She glanced at me, then patted Sally on the arm. 'I'll be here for another half-hour if you need anything.'

After she left, Sally pushed up the sleeves of her sweatshirt. 'Actually, there is one thing I remembered,' she said, speaking so softly that I had to lean closer to hear. 'I could smell perfume, I think it was perfume, or it might have been that body spray stuff.'

'Did you tell the police?'

'No, I only thought about it when I was lying in bed last night. It's funny how you can remember smells, or sometimes you smell something and it reminds you...

James had some aftershave for Christmas, from one of our aunts. He said it smelt like a—' She broke off, glancing at the door. 'I don't think Mummy will come down. She didn't really want me to see a psychiatrist.'

'I'm not a psychiatrist,' I said. 'A psychologist's different. There's nothing the matter with you, Sally, I'm just here to try and help you so whoever it was in the car doesn't get the chance to do something like that again. This perfume, you say it reminded you of James's aftershave?'

'No, I only meant it had that horrible sharp smell that hurts your nose. Anyway, James threw it in the bin.'

'So you couldn't actually give it a name?'

She shook her head. She looked close to tears. 'That girl that disappeared a few weeks ago,' she said, 'is she dead?'

There was no point in falsely reassuring her. 'No one knows what's happened to her, I'm afraid.'

'But if I can't remember they might... Anyway, with that girl it was different. She was older than me, and pretty.'

'Who told you that?'

'I did.' The voice came from outside, in the entrance hall, but a moment later

24

a head came round the door.

'Oh, it's you.' Her brother's arrival seemed to have done nothing to make Sally feel more at ease. If anything it had had the opposite effect. 'This is the lady who's—'

'Yes, I know who it is.' James was walking round the room, lifting things up, then putting them down. From the look of his hair he had only just got out of bed, but if anything his dishevelled appearance enhanced rather than detracted from his good looks. If his colouring had been dark his high cheekbones and rather narrow eyes would have made him look almost oriental. His nose was similar to Sally's—small and slightly upturned—but everything else about him was more extreme. Fairer hair, bluer eyes, sharper jawline. He was wearing jeans that had worn through just below the knees and across the back of one thigh, and a pair of battered white trainers with no laces. A red towel, hanging round his neck, only partially covered his smooth, bare chest.

When he turned to face me his expression was studiously bored. 'Give it a rest now, can you? She's told the pigs everything she knows. Anyway what's the point? Have you any idea what their clear-up rate is?' He stared at me, his head slightly tilted back, his voice was full of scorn. 'OK, for homicide it's around ninety per cent, but overall it's nearer fifteen.'

'Where did you read that?' He was right, as a matter of fact, but that only served to make his supercilious manner even more annoying.

'Look, I hope this visit's a one-off,' he said, resting his arm on the mantelpiece and nearly dislodging an expensive-looking china vase. 'Is anyone actually concerned about my sister's state of mind, or is she just part of a pointless investigation to justify the pigs receiving their pay cheques at the end of the month? Wouldn't you say Sally's been through enough already? It's only six months since our father died.'

'I'm sorry.'

'You're sorry.' His face flushed with anger. 'Look, my mother's ill so I have a perfect right to stay with Sally while you—'

'Absolutely, but it would be easier if you sat down.'

'Why? Why do I have to sit down?' He looked briefly in the direction of Sally, who now had part of her sweatshirt stuffed in her mouth, then strolled across the room, whistling through his teeth, slid open the patio door and stepped into the garden. 'Look, I don't know what special techniques you shrinks use, but whatever they are you're wasting your time. If Sally'd remembered anything new she'd have told me and I'd have passed it on.'

'She remembered the smell of perfume,' I said.

'Oh, that.'

Sally was watching him anxiously. The scab on her leg had started to bleed. She rubbed at it, then licked her finger. 'I told her,' she said, jerking her head in my direction, 'about it being a bit like that aftershave Auntie Eleanor gave you.'

James snorted. 'Right. Good. Now they'll think it was me in the car.' Then he saw her face. 'Oh, don't be such an idiot.' He turned towards me. 'Look, my mother hasn't been well, not since the accident.' He spoke the word *accident* with heavy sarcasm, then noticed my puzzled expression. 'Oh, I'm not talking about what happened to Sally. They haven't told you about my father's death, then? An unfortunate accident. Yes, well, it's always so much easier to call it an accident, close the file, shove it in a cupboard, and get on with more important matters, like checking road tax discs and handing out parking tickets.'

He was walking away. I followed him on to the patio.

'You think there was something suspicious about your father's death? But why would anyone have wanted to harm him?'

He was standing very still, with his back turned. 'You never met him,' he said angrily. 'If you had you wouldn't ask such a bloody silly question.'

Fifteen minutes later, driving across the Downs, I became aware that the car behind, an old mustard-coloured Capri, was much too close to my rear bumper. I flicked on my lights, slowing down but not so much that the driver had no time to react, then watched in my driving mirror as he pulled out to overtake, raced past, then almost lost control on the bend. When I reached the main road the Capri was parked on a strip of grass, near the zoo, and the driver had his head down, nodding in time to the music that was blaring through his window. Catching a glimpse of his profile, I had no difficulty recognizing the thick fair hair, high cheekbones and slightly upturned nose. Presumably that was what he intended me to do.

Chapter Three

'Anna? Didn't expect to see you here.' Graham Whittle was out of breath and had to pause between words. During the seven or eight months since we had last met he had lost weight. Now that his face was thinner his nose looked slightly more hooked and his eyes a little deeper set, and I remembered how he had once told me he had an Italian mother.

'Stepped out of the car,' he said, 'and saw a kid nicking plants from outside the garden centre.'

'Caught him?'

'Her. No, far too quick for me.' He wiped his forehead with the sleeve of his shirt. 'Oh, you're here about the little girl who was almost dragged into a car. Gave her the third degree, did you? No, don't tell me, we buggered it up and you had to pick up the pieces.' He winked at the desk sergeant. 'Howard's in his room, only I'd treat him with a fair amount of caution if I were you, hasn't been in the best of moods these last few days.'

I could see Howard Fry coming out of his office. When he spotted me he glanced at his watch, then turned back and held open his door, tapping his foot as he waited for me to walk the length of the corridor.

'Ten minutes,' he announced.

'Likewise,' I said.

He managed a feeble smile. 'Sorry. Meeting with the Assistant Chief Constable. Sally Luckham—how did it go?'

The room smelled faintly of cigarettes. He must have just seen off another visitor, and if he had allowed him to smoke it must have been someone important. Howard had given up three or four years ago, and still had the condemnatory attitude of a reformed smoker. I knew the feeling.

'It's an odd family,' I said. 'Actually, the mother was in bed all the time I was there and I only had the pleasure of the brother's company for five minutes or so.' I had decided not to mention the incident on the Downs: James warning me to stay away from his sister, or else. 'Why didn't you tell me their father only died a few months ago? What happened? Was there something odd about it? James mentioned an accident, and he doesn't seem too enamoured of you lot.'

Howard had his back turned, searching for something in his filing cabinet. 'Thought you'd have read about the case,' he said, straightening up, then smoothing down the dark red hair that was receding at the temples but had been allowed to grow a little longer at the back. What was it about dead straight hair? A conditioned response to some early sexual experience?

'He was a diabetic,' he said. 'Got stranded up on the Mendips.'

'Oh, yes.' The way he put it made it sound like the two things went together.

'God knows what happened. As far as anyone could tell he'd climbed up Secker Gorge, then slipped off the rocks at the top, fallen and broken both his legs. He wasn't found for quite a time. His car had been parked in a lay-by, that's what led us to the body.'

'Couldn't he have dragged himself to a place where someone would see him?'

'Have you ever been to Secker Gorge? Anyway, it wasn't the injuries that killed him, or the cold. Diabetic coma. Doctor thought he must have left home in a hurry, had his insulin injection, but failed to eat a proper breakfast. Of course, by the time he was found it was impossible to tell exactly what had happened.'

'Surcly he'd have carried glucose tablets.'

Howard nodded slowly. 'You'd have thought so. A colleague of mine, with a wife who has a tendency to suffer sudden attacks, has been issued with glucogen injections, not that it would have been much use in Luckham's case. He was on his own.'

'How d'you know?'

He sat down, still without looking at her. 'Cut out any ideas like that, Anna. The coroner decided there was nothing untoward.'

'I'm not suggesting there was.' I felt annoyed that I had been asked to visit a family that had undergone such a traumatic experience, without anyone bothering to put me in the picture. Howard was leaning back with his eyes half closed. He seemed to have forgotten about the Assistant Chief Constable, but more than likely the appointment was not for another hour—he had just felt the need to impress on me how desperately busy, and by implication how desperately important he was. No, that wasn't Howard's style. I was over reacting, on edge because my interview with Sally had produced so little.

'If I'd told you about it before,' he said, 'you'd have gone to the house with all kinds of preconceived ideas. I wanted you to have an open mind. Anyway, forget about all that, have your special techniques enabled the girl to remember a few solid facts?'

Special techniques. He sounded almost as sceptical as James Luckham. 'She's frightened,' I said, 'but there's something else. I've a definite feeling she knows more than she's letting on. Today it was mainly a question of gaining her confidence.'

'Look, I don't want to tell you how to do your job.' He fiddled with the pen on his desk. 'But there's a fourteen-year-old girl who could be lying face down in a ditch. I was hoping one visit to the Luckham house would have been enough.'

Outside in the corridor some kind of scuffle was going on. Voices were raised, Howard's door received a kick, then the sounds started to fade as whoever was making them was escorted towards the cells.

'The missing girl, Geena Robson,' I said, 'what was she like?'

'Do you mean, why are we so worried about her? Partly, the fact that she was seen being pulled into a car, although I suppose it's possible the account of what happened was exaggerated. But it's not just that. She doesn't sound the type to have run off without saying a word to anyone. According to her relatives and teachers she's a quiet, introverted sort of girl, with no boyfriend and few interests outside her school work. She and her mother live in a small flat over a second-hand bookshop and her mother has a part-time job walking round Broadmead shopping centre trying to persuade people to agree to have a mail order catalogue sent to their house.'

'And you say the father lives with another woman?'

He nodded. 'We checked all that. It was the obvious conclusion when she first went missing. A dispute over custody or access, although by the time kids are fourteen all that kind of thing's usually over and done with.'

Howard's son was younger than that. I wondered if the two of them were still in touch on a regular basis, or if the divorce had meant the boy and his mother had moved to another part of the country.

'You mean Geena Robson would have made up her own mind if and when she wanted to see her father?' I asked. 'Incidentally, Sally Luckham says she thinks she smelled perfume.'

'That's what she told you? Any particular brand?'

'She didn't know, said it had reminded her of some aftershave an aunt had given to her brother.'

Howard raised his eyebrows. 'Perfume, aftershave, can anyone be certain they can tell the difference?'

'Aftershave usually smells...' I searched for the right word. 'Stronger, muskier.'

'She never mentioned it to Ritsema.'

'No.'

Howard pulled a face. 'You've never met him but already you've got him down as an insensitive slob who browbeats little girls into silence. When are you seeing her again? There's a strong possibility she read about the missing girl in the local paper and decided inventing an attempted abduction would be a good way of getting a bit of attention.'

'Oh, I'm sure that's not right.'

He lifted a briefcase onto the desk, then stood up. 'That would account for her

36

attack of nerves and the fact that even you think she's hiding something. If you want my opinion, she's wishing she'd never started it. Still, for the time being we'll have to take it at face value.' He opened a drawer and started taking out papers and slipping them into a folder. 'How's Owen?'

The sudden change of subject threw me a little. 'Owen? He's fine. At least as far as I know he is. He's in Melbourne, on an exchange with another academic.'

'The other man's come to Bristol?'

'Woman. She's called Fay Somers.'

'Must feel strange all alone in the flat. Going to bed on your own, that's when it really hits home.' He looked up, not smiling, just checking to make sure I realized he was talking about himself. 'You know, if Sally Luckham really does know something it could give us the breakthrough we've been waiting for. On the other hand, if you can persuade her to admit she's been leading us on a wild goose chase, at least we can eliminate her and get on with our other enquiries.'

I could hear Nick talking to Heather. The sash cord on the waiting room window had finally snapped. So, by the sound of it, had Heather. Or was it something to do with Dawn?

Dawn Rivers. Was it her fault she had a name like a country and western singer? She had only been working with us for a couple of weeks—brought in as a temporary replacement when Martin developed shingles and was ordered to take a month off sick—but it had been a tough two weeks. Nick would only admit to finding her mildly irritating, but Heather was on my side. Perhaps Dawn was just one of those people women find it hard to like. Heather thought men might find her sexy in a 'strict nanny' kind of way but I doubted if this had anything to do with my aversion towards her. Maybe Dawn's super-efficiency was making me uneasy? If I was absolutely honest with myself, would I have liked to deal with clients in the brisk, know-all way she seemed to favour? Not that any of us had actually seen her with a client. Maybe she was warm and empathic, reserving her off-putting manner for her colleagues.

I heard her coming out of her room and made a decision to start afresh, make a real effort to acknowledge her good points.

'Oh, I was hoping to catch you, Dawn.' *If you want to make someone feel good ask their advice.* 'Didn't you say you'd read a paper on hyperventilating? Only this man came in, gasping for air, and—'

'I'll bring it in for you,' she said, taking an electronic notebook from her bag, flicking open the cover, then operating the pocket-sized keyboard with lightning speed. Her clothes were as severe as her tone of voice: dark jacket and skirt, white shirt, navy shoes.

'By the way,' she said, still keeping her eyes on the notebook, 'that boy you've been seeing, the one with big boots and an earring, can't keep his next appointment.'

'Did he make another?'

'Mmm? No, I don't think so. He just walked into the building, happened to see me coming out of Heather's office and gave me some garbled message about how he had to see a friend.'

'Lloyd,' said Heather, who must have been listening to the conversation from behind the office door. 'Don't worry, Anna, I'll give him a ring. Nice boy, very polite.'

Nick had disappeared. He couldn't handle the tension between me and Dawn, but I wasn't going to let him opt out that easily, and he knew it. When I tapped on his door he was waiting for me.

'Look, Anna, she's only here for another two or three weeks.'

'Martin could be away for months.'

'With shingles?'

'It's the chicken pox virus,' I said. 'It reappears when you're under stress.'

Nick sighed. 'So what d'you want me to do?'

He looked so exasperated I couldn't keep a straight face. 'Listen,' I said, 'I've been seeing this girl who was almost abducted on her way home from school. Someone tried to pull her into a car, but she managed to bite her attacker, struggle free and run off.'

'Really? Who referred her?'

'No, she's not a client. Howard Fry. Actually the guy in charge of the case is called Ritsema. He's new to the area and, as far as I can tell, fairly heavy-handed.'

'So Howard called you in to pour oil on troubled waters.'

'The girl's father was called Tom Luckham. Can you remember reading about him? Apparently he went for a walk on the Mendips, injured himself pretty badly, then lapsed into a diabetic coma.'

Nick thought about it. 'Yes, I do remember vaguely. Wasn't he an artist or something? How old was he?'

'I'm not sure. Forty, fifty?'

'What was he doing on the Mendips? Wouldn't he have told someone where he was going? So you think his daughter could've made up the abduction story because she can't come to terms with her father's death?'

I opened my mouth to say it was a possibility, but he hadn't finished.

'Sudden death of a loved one,' he said, 'doesn't fit into our representation of the world, makes us want to find a reason.'

'Yes, I know.' Since his mother's fatal stroke he had become increasingly absorbed with how people adjusted to the loss of someone close to them. It worried me a little. He was even thinking of writing a paper about grief and psychosomatic illness. It was verging on an obsession.

'The trouble is,' I said, moving the conversation back to Sally Luckham, 'I'm supposed to find out if she's telling the truth and, if so, try and get her to describe her attacker in a little more detail, or at

41

least remember the colour of the car.'

'Yes, I see.' Nick had taken a book off his shelf. 'Has she mentioned her father's accident? If not, it's probably because she's still at the *why me* stage. We all like to feel we're more or less in control of our lives. An unexpected death reminds us how wrong we are.'

'Yes, all right Nick.' Prior to my visit to the Luckham house I had been fighting off depression. For some reason, working alongside the police had cheered me up, although Howard asking about Owen had reminded me how insecure I felt about the relationship. He had been away before, of course, but only for two or three nights, and while he was gone I had vowed I would never find fault with him again. Then, within an hour or two of his return the doubts had returned. Did I really want to spend the rest of my life with someone who thought delving into the way people felt did more harm than good? Someone who boasted that he couldn't remember crying, not since he was a small boy and fell out of a tree. Not even when his wife died?

'Luckham,' said Nick. 'Yes, I remember. The case prompted a phone-in on one of the local radio stations, some doctor answering questions about the difference between diabetic and hypoglycaemic comas, too little insulin or too much.'

'Apparently strenuous exercise can affect the blood sugar level.'

'Yes, that's right. Anyway, what was he doing, this Luckham bloke? He was found at Secker Gorge, am I right? There's a path that goes down to the bottom, then gradually winds up to a kind of rocky plateau. You'd hate it, Anna. Like all people who suffer from vertigo you'd have an irresistible urge to hurl yourself from the top!' He smiled, then his expression changed, but I still wasn't sure if he was being serious or just trying to take my mind off Dawn Rivers. 'Of course, he could've been pushed.'

The new client, booked in to see me at two-fifteen, was something of a celebrity. Perhaps that was the wrong word. His face had made the nationals, the same photograph reproduced whenever another chapter in the story unfolded. Stephen Bryce, a vicar in his mid-thirties, kicked out of his parish in Bristol because of his unorthodox views on the nature of

God. Had the bishop made the decision against Bryce's wishes or had he left of his own free-will? According to the media the parish was split down the middle, with some of the parishioners agreeing with the bishop, others seeing Bryce as some kind of hero.

I tried to recall his picture but got stuck with the eyes so that the rest of the face became a blur. Small, intense eyes, although probably not as dark as they looked in the newspaper. A beard? Yes, he definitely had a beard, although that might have gone now, along with the dog collar and clerical dress.

When I found him in the waiting room he was both like his photo and very different. Hair not so black, eyes not so small. No beard.

He stood up, as if he recognized me, although we had never met before. 'Dr McColl? I'm afraid I got here rather early. I wasn't sure how long it would take me to find you.'

'No, it's not all that easy, and the traffic can be terrible. If you'd like to come this way.' We shook hands and started up the stairs.

'Actually I walked,' he said.

'All the way from Kingsdown?'

He gave a short laugh. 'Time hangs heavy, I was glad of the fresh air, if you can call it that.'

When we entered my room he looked all round, as if he was checking it against some preconceived notion of how a psychologist's room ought to be. 'I had no idea what you'd be like,' he said, 'but we got off to a good start when I spoke to you on the phone and you didn't call me reverend.'

'My father's a church warden,' I said. 'Do sit down.'

'Right. Thank you.' He was wearing a dark open-neck shirt and black cord trousers. I wondered if he had abandoned his dog collar when he left the parish, or perhaps he had been the kind of priest who prefers not to wear clerical dress. He was fairly short, but of average build, with a long, thin face and now that his beard had been shaved off it was possible to speculate that he had grown it to hide a rather pock-marked complexion, suggesting he had suffered from acne as an adolescent. His deep-set eyes had the restless, intense look of someone who has strongly held opinions, and possibly a quick temper, but has

45

learned how to keep a tight control of his emotions.

'I'd better tell you straight away,' he announced. 'I'm really here on behalf of my wife.'

'She asked you to come.'

'Oh no, she'd never have done that, but I'm worried about her, I think she may need some professional help. Things haven't been easy during the last few months.' He broke off, frowning. 'I'm sorry, I'm assuming you know something about me.'

'Only what I've read in the newspaper.'

'Yes, well in that case you won't be surprised to hear we've had to move out of the vicarage. Not that I'm blaming anyone for that. The bishop couldn't have been more considerate, impressing on us that he was quite happy to let us stay as long as it took to fix up something reasonably permanent, but Ros preferred to leave as quickly as possible.'

'Yes I can understand that. You've found somewhere else?'

'Ros is staying with a friend, well, not a friend exactly, more of an acquaintance, in a village between Bristol and Bath. I'm—well, just at this point in time

I'm in what was described as a studio apartment, but is actually one large room with a kitchenette.' He stood up and started walking backwards and forwards. 'I'm sorry, I'm not explaining things very well. The marriage is over, beyond retrieval. I've let her down. In fact, looking back, I've been incredibly selfish.'

He paused. Waiting for me to contradict him? When I said nothing he repeated himself. 'Totally selfish, self-obsessed.'

'Aren't you being rather hard on yourself?'

'You think so? At the time the book came out I'm not sure I even considered the effect on Ros.'

'She knew what it was about?'

'Oh, yes, yes of course, but I don't think either of us realized the effect it was going to have.'

There was something slightly theatrical about him. It would have been unfair to say he was putting on an act, but his concern for his wife didn't quite ring true. Still, like actors, vicars are expected to hold an audience. After a time, it probably comes naturally to them.

'Shall we start at the beginning?' I said. 'All I know is that you gave up your parish after the bishop objected to a book you wrote.'

He sat down again, then leaned forward, resting his hands on his knees. '*God is Good,* that was the title of the book. To tell you the truth, I had no idea it was going to cause such a stir. Hardly a new idea: God as perfect goodness, perfect understanding, rather than an old man up in the sky.'

'More like Eastern religion,' I said, but now was not the time for a theological discussion, however enjoyable it might have been. As it was, I was having to make quite an effort to allow him to tell me what had happened in his own way; I had been longing to hear the whole inside story.

'Of course, all religions have their own myths and metaphors,' he said, 'in keeping with the culture of the people who belong to them. Ros agrees with me, well, up to a point she does, but it was different for her. Does faith have anything to do with Jesus as a historical figure?' The somewhat dramatic tone of voice had been replaced by a kind of tortured whine. 'The wife of a clergyman is expected to go to all kinds of ridiculous functions, mostly attended by people—' He broke off, his eyes meeting mine, then looked away. 'No, I don't want to sound like a cold intellectual, although I suppose that's exactly what I am. Ros is more gregarious, far better suited to the job of a parish priest.'

'I doubt if it's quite that simple,' I said. 'Look, I hope you don't mind me asking, but were you forced out of your parish or was it your own decision to leave?'

He hesitated, but only for a moment. 'Oh, it was by mutual agreement, after a fair amount of soul-searching on both sides. I've no regrets, well, hardly any, apart from the pain it's caused Ros.'

'There must be practical problems, too, like how you're going to earn a living.'

'Yes, of course, but I've enough money put aside to provide for Ros, at least for the time being. The trouble is, I'm afraid anything I say or do will only make matters worse. I suppose that's where you come in, I need your advice. No, don't tell me, psychologists don't give advice, even I know that.'

Out in the street the traffic had come to a stop and the exhaust from an ancient pick-up truck was blackening the air. An old woman with a basket on wheels was crossing the road at a dangerously slow pace.

'You wanted to talk over the situation with someone who can be more objective,' I said, 'and you didn't think your wife would be prepared to come here with you.'

'The two of us?' He looked appalled at the suggestion. 'I should think it's the last thing she'd want.'

'You say she's staying with a friend?'

'Livvy, Livvy Pope. I suppose her real name's Olivia. She writes poetry.'

'The two of you felt you needed some time alone, away from each other?'

'Sorry?' He had heard what I said, but was playing for time. 'Yes. No, there's very little chance of us getting back together again.' I could see the top of his head, where his hair had started to thin a little. 'I was never cut out for the Church,' he said. 'Sometimes I wonder what I was thinking about. No, maybe that's not right. Maybe I've changed.' He looked up, and smiled a little sheepishly. 'Sorry, I came to talk about my wife and here I am, indulging in more tedious introspection.'

'Don't you think if she wanted to talk to someone your wife could have arranged it herself?'

His hands were gripping the arms of his chair. 'So what you're saying is I'm here just to get myself off the hook, stop myself feeling so guilty? I tell you what, I'll write her a note, tell her if she needs to talk to someone...' He glanced at the clock. 'How long am I allowed? Another twenty minutes or so? He moved his chair a little closer to mine. 'You see, there's something else. I'm not sure how to put this. You may feel... You see, Tom Luckham, Sally's father, was one of my parishioners. You probably know that already.'

'No, I didn't,' I said, irritated that it now looked as if he had made the appointment in order to pump me for information about Sally.

'I'm sorry.' He had guessed what I was thinking. 'You must feel I'm wasting your time, indulging in aimless gossip, but it's not like that.'

'Who told you I'd been to see Sally?'

'Yes, I should have explained. I phoned Erica, Sally's mother, just to see how she was and she said a Dr McColl had been round, sent by the CID. I'd no idea you did work for the police, but of course it makes sense in a case like that.'

'Was there something you were going to

tell me, about Sally's father?'

He drew in a deep breath, then let it out again in a long, despairing sigh. 'Ever since he died... Look, I'd better explain. He was probably my closest friend, even though we were about as different as you can get. D'you believe in altruism? I used to, now I'm not so sure. One of those questions it's impossible to resolve. Do we put money in a collecting box because we feel sympathy for those worse off than ourselves, or as a superstitious gesture designed to appease the gods?'

'If we give to the blind we won't go blind?'

'Exactly.' He was rubbing his hands together. They were small and narrow. He still had a ring on his wedding finger. 'Ros blamed Tom for my decision to give up the parish.'

'Why would she do that?'

'I suppose it was easier than blaming me. And more humiliating. She likes to make out I was too much under Tom's influence. He believed the role of the parish priest was to alleviate suffering, not get caught up in pointless arguments about concepts of God. As I said, I'm not very good with people, never have been. An academic, I might've been quite successful at that.' He paused, and I could see by the rise and fall of his chest that his breathing had become rapid, shallow. 'The day Tom died... I don't know how much you've heard. Apparently someone rang quite early in the morning. Apart from Tom everyone was still in bed, but Sally heard the phone, and as far as she could remember the call came at about seven-fifteen. Tom didn't need much sleep so he'd probably have been up and about. I expect you know he was a diabetic, but as far as his health was concerned, and it was the same with everything else, he was meticulous. He'd never have risked a hypoglycaemic attack.'

'Unless the phone call was something very urgent,' I said. 'No one ever discovered who'd made it?'

He rubbed his chin and I wondered if there was something symbolic about the removal of his beard. 'The police made enquiries,' he said, 'but if it was from a phone box there was no way of checking. I was up in London all day, I'd gone in the car, to visit some specialist bookshops. When I got back that evening... Somehow it made it worse, not knowing exactly what happened, and inevitably it led to all kinds of speculation and rumour.' He paused, giving me a long, unblinking stare. 'The attack on Sally,' he said, 'do you think it's remotely possible it was linked in some way with her father's death?'

'I'm not sure I quite understand what you're saying. Tom Luckham's death was an accident. He injured himself, then went into a coma.'

'No, it couldn't have been an accident. It's not just me. Didn't Sally say anything? And James, her brother, he's as convinced as I am.' He had jumped up and was standing with his hands on the back of his chair. 'Tom would never have let it happen. If you'd met him you'd know I was right.'

Chapter Four

Friday morning and my least favourite client was due at any moment. The flowers came through the door first, an absurdly large bunch, wrapped in cellophane, although I knew they had been picked from Mrs Priestly's garden.

'Put them in water,' she ordered, 'the stems don't need trimming but it might be best if I arrange them for you.' She glanced at her last offering, a bouquet of yellow roses, squeezed into a jug Heather had found in the cupboard under the stairs. 'Here, give me those, they're dead as doornails.'

Stuffing the old flowers in the rubbish bin, she began arranging the new ones, talking all the while about the shortcomings of her daughter-in-law and grandchildren. 'Matthew, he's the eldest, when his father was still at home I had high hopes of the boy. Now...' She turned her head, lifting her shoulders, then letting them drop dramatically. 'Jennifer just doesn't know how to handle him. And as for Rachel—'

'She's the four-year-old?' I interrupted. 'It must be difficult for you and your daughter-in-law now your son's gone back to London.'

It was quite common for clients to come asking for advice, not for themselves, but for a relative or friend. Wasn't that exactly what Stephen Bryce had done, although in his case he had also wanted to find out how much I knew about Sally Luckham's attempted abduction, and to try to convince me there was something suspicious about Tom Luckham's death. According to James, Sally was suffering from tonsillitis. I would like to have gone round to the house and talked to her in bed. People who feel slightly unwell are often less defensive; sinking into the role of a patient makes them feel more childlike, more dependent. What was I thinking about? Sally Luckham *was* a child. The tonsillitis was almost certainly an invention, designed to protect Sally from more questions, but I could hardly accuse James of lying, and in any case what good would it have done? I could have asked to speak to Mrs Luckham—surely she wanted the 'abductor' apprehended, if only for the sake of other children in the area—but in the event I had accepted James's story and told him I would ring back the following day.

The flower arrangement was complete. Mrs Priestly sat down heavily. 'If Jennifer had been a better wife and mother it would never have happened, Gavin leaving. Well, to be perfectly honest, some people used to wonder why he'd stayed as long as he did.'

'What people?' My question had just slipped out, but its significance was not lost on Mrs Priestly.

She smiled insincerely, then gave me a slightly pitying look. 'Everyone who knew the two of them, my dear. I know you want to help but I sometimes feel you haven't quite grasped the picture. Now if I tell you about Matthew's school.'

All I could think about was poor Jennifer whose husband had left her with three children to look after, and his seventy-year-old mother in a flat just down the road.

'Matthew,' she repeated, 'is exceptionally intelligent but I don't feel he's receiving sufficient stimulation. I wanted Jennifer to insist on having him tested to establish how gifted he is, but she says as long as he's happy...'

After Mrs Priestly left, Heather buzzed to say a parcel with my name on it had arrived in the second post. Down in the office she handed it to me, barely able to contain her curiosity.

'Looks like wedding cake, Anna. If you don't like marzipan...'

'You're welcome to it,' I said, 'but it's more likely to be one of those "How to Give up Smoking" or "How to Control your Nerves" cassettes. There's this guy in Wolverhampton who sends them out by the score in the hope that we'll give his name and address to clients.'

The small package was bound with about two feet of sticky tape. I started tearing at the paper with my teeth, but Heather gave me a disapproving look, found a pair of scissors and snipped through one end of the package. She was dressed in white trousers and an enormous T-shirt with Van Gogh's *Sunflowers* on the front. Normally she never wore trousers—one of her teenage daughters had made some remark about the size of her hips—but Kieran moving in with the three of them seemed to have had a good effect. She was happier, more confident, her self-image had been raised a couple of notches.

'Seen Dawn?' I asked.

Heather pulled a face. 'Dr Ingram referred a girl with eating problems. Dawn told her to keep a diary of everything she ate.'

'How d'you know?'

'She asked if I had a notebook she could give the girl. You wouldn't have done that, would you, Anna? When Selina got silly about her diet you told me to avoid talking about food and to try and find out if there was something bothering her.'

'Different people have different methods,' I said. 'Look, I was right about the cassette, but since it's been recorded by the sender and the label's blank, it's impossible to tell what's on it.'

'Want to have a listen?' Heather opened a cupboard and took out an ancient tape recorder. 'Or perhaps it's private?'

'Put it in,' I said. 'If it was *that* private, whoever sent it would have enclosed his name and address.'

It started with a short solo on an electronic keyboard, then a guitar joined in, and finally the voice of the lead singer, accompanied by a chorus of 'Oh, yeahs.'

You've taken enough. She's taken it all. Tell her this is the end, the end, the end. Your life in her hands, but you've taken enough. Tell her this is the end, say enough is enough.

Heather turned down the volume. 'Any idea who could've sent it?'

'Haven't a clue.'

'Think I might have heard Selina playing it, but they all sound much the same, don't they?'

The singer's voice had become a low growl. *Hit back hard, do it now. I don't care what they say. With her life in my hands, they can lock me away.*

Before Owen left for Australia I had promised to get in touch with Fay Somers, the visiting academic who was coming to the university to work with someone who was writing a book on child development. I knew nothing about her—Owen had met her once but was unable to recall the slightest detail, apart from the fact that she had rather a loud voice—but in half an hour's time I would find out more.

We had fixed to meet at a pub in Whiteladies Road. Fay had been there before, with the woman who owned the house in Eastbury where she was renting

60

an attic flat, and, if our phone conversation was anything to go by, she already knew more about the local pubs than I had discovered in several years. She seemed to be one of those people who insist on telling you every detail about their circumstances. *The owners of the house are called Jill and Tony Hinchcliffe, Anna.* She used my name in every other sentence. *Tony works for a bank and Jill runs a day nursery that gives priority to children from problem families. My research is mainly Child Development, with an emphasis on older kids, rather than young babies.* She had promised to tell me more when we met.

The walk from Cliftonwood to White-ladies Road always took longer than I expected, so by the time I reached the pub it was crowded out. Pausing, with my hand on the door, looking up at the hanging baskets, I tried to recall the description Fay had given me over the phone. *Average weight, average height, curly brown hair that's not so dark, not so light, roundish face.* Not much to go on, but if she was as extrovert as she sounded she had probably struck up a conversation with the barman and I would recognize the accent.

The area by the bar was packed. I stood on tiptoe, peering over the seething mass of heads, but there was no sign of anyone answering Fay's description. A huge man, in an extremely unattractive pair of tartan shorts, was trying to attract the attention of the barman, while fending off a group of students who were attempting to push their way through. Then someone tapped me on the shoulder.

'Anna?'

'Fay?' When I spoke her name she responded like an eager child.

'I guessed the way you were looking all around it must be you. Good to meet you, what are you having?'

All the seats were taken, but a smoochy-looking couple appeared to be disentangling themselves, prior to leaving. I started ordering the drinks, then suggested Fay grabbed the two vacant seats.

'Good idea, only do let me pay. The next round then. Have you eaten? I had something before I came out but if you're hungry I've heard they do a real good chilli con carne. Oh, what am I talking about, I expect you've been here heaps of times. It's probably your local.'

When I joined her she already had her

lips slightly parted, waiting to speak. 'It was so kind of you to give me a call.' She took both glasses and placed them on the cardboard mats. 'I only met Owen once. Four years ago, it was, when I was working in Canberra.'

'You're based in Sydney now?'

'Been there a couple of years.'

'I have a brother living in Sydney,' I said, 'but I've only visited once, just for a couple of weeks.'

'Really? So you've seen the Opera House, botanical gardens, Bondi Beach. Did you have a chance to get out in the countryside at all? Katoomba, up in the mountains, now there's a place you'd love, and if you'd carried on, through Bathhurst and Dubbo... I had a friend who worked as a supply teacher, in a place called Cobar. Fantastic, miles from anywhere. A dead straight road that just keeps on and on...' She broke off, but only to draw breath. 'Tell me about your brother. How long's he been out there? What does he do for a living?'

'Nothing to tell really. He's married, couple of kids. Works for a large engineering company.'

'You have other brothers and sisters?

Parents living not too far away?'

'My father lives in Kent, quite near London. My mother died five years ago.'

'Oh, I'm sorry.' She sounded as if she meant it. 'My parents split when I was still at school and they've both remarried, but we're on pretty good terms, although it can be heartbreaking imagining how things might have been if they'd stayed together.'

'Yes, I'm sure.' She was so friendly, so direct, what must she have made of Owen and his strenuous efforts to avoid talking about anything that might elicit strong feelings? Come to think of it, what was she making of me?

Soon after, I managed to steer the conversation round to her latest research project. 'Owen said you work with families. It sounds interesting.'

She lifted her glass and took a sip of lager, nodding appreciatively.

'That's right. My latest project's on parental attachment. Most parents—well, I'd say it's strongest in the female—are prepared to go to almost any lengths to protect their infant.' She put up both hands, slapping her own cheeks. 'What am I talking about, you're a psych. grad.

yourself and here's me—'

'No, carry on. I'd like to hear.'

'Self-sacrifice,' she said. 'Is there such a thing or is behaviour that seems altruistic really an illusion?'

'Yes, I know what you mean.' Was this to be a re-run of my conversation with Stephen Bryce? 'Funnily enough, I was discussing exactly that question with a client—'

'Really? That's amazing. Your job, you know you're going to have to tell me all about it. The place where I'm staying in Eastbury, they're sweet people. Two kids, eleven and nine, lovely ages. And their mother, Jill, she's a wonderful person and really interested in counselling and psychotherapy. Did I tell you, she runs this day nursery for the kids of single mothers? Apparently one of the little girls is way ahead in her development. Jill wanted her given some kind of test—by an Ed. Psych., I suppose—but I wasn't too sure.'

I glanced at the menu on a board on the wall, not certain if I was hungry or if the thought of food was repugnant. I had eaten nothing since lunch, and even that had only consisted of a stale cheese roll. Owen often complained that my bad temper was the result of not eating enough, but if I ordered something now Fay would feel bad about having eaten before she came out. A man standing by the bar looked rather like Stephen Bryce. Same dark hair, slightly hunched shoulders, but when he turned to speak to a friend, his big, bulbous nose and large, vacant-looking eyes couldn't have been more different. Why had Stephen seemed so determined to convince me that Tom Luckham's death had not been an accident? Even if I believed him, what on earth was I supposed to do? My connection with the Luckham family was unlikely to last longer than a week. I felt sorry for Sally, but as Howard was fond of pointing out, my job was to drag more information out of her, not start treating her like one of my clients.

'How would you feel about it, Anna?' Fay was still talking about the gifted child.

'I'd say, leave the kid in peace, at least till she's at primary school.'

'Oh, me too. You know the worst thing in the world is to grow up with everyone having such expectations, and feeling whatever you do can never live up to them.'

'You sound as if you're talking from experience,' I said.

She blushed at little. 'Oh, you know how it is, doting mother, every duckling a swan. Of course, *my* main interest is teenagers and their parents. Does the mother have a different attitude from the father? Does the attitude depend on the gender of the kid? I used to work in health psychology, mainly looking at teenage non-compliance in taking medication. You know the kind of things—epilepsy, diabetes. Non-compliance, what a terrible expression. If you were a fifteen-year-old kid would you want your mother nagging you about blood tests, telling you what you can and can't eat?'

She broke off suddenly, apologizing for talking too much, unaware that she had my rapt attention.

'So you know quite a bit about diabetes,' I said.

She looked at me curiously. 'Oh, I wouldn't say that. Just the basics.'

'If someone gave themselves an insulin injection, then missed a meal, could it be fatal?'

'Unlikely. A patient in insulin shock needs sugar fast. In fact you could say a brain deprived of sugar is as much at risk as a brain deprived of oxygen, but all diabetics carry glucose tablets, or some such equivalent. The patient would notice the symptoms of hypoglycaemia —headache, dizziness, irritability—and take steps to counteract the attack. Given sugar, even a comatose patient wakes up in seconds. You have some special reason for wanting to know?'

'A man who died last January. No, not someone I knew. A relative of a client.'

'Tragic. In my experience diabetics fall into two categories: those who take good care of themselves, and those who go through phases of feeling so sore about their condition they don't keep a proper check on their blood sugar levels and let their diet go to pieces.'

'This man was meticulous about his treatment, or so I've been told. He'd gone out for a walk on the Mendips.'

'The Mendips?'

'Sorry, it's a range of hills to the south of the city. There's a large gorge—Cheddar Gorge—with caves you can visit, and a place called Wookey Hole—'

'Sounds great. You can get there in a car or d'you have to go on foot?'

'Oh, Cheddar and Wookey are tourist attractions, but the gorge where this man was walking is more off the beaten track, although you can drive there if you don't mind the bumps in the road.'

'He was on his own?'

'It seems so,' I said. 'Verdict of death by misadventure, but...'

'You're wondering why he would have put himself at risk, allowed himself to go into a coma in the middle of nowhere.' She patted my hand. 'Listen, you must come round to the flat, meet Jill and Tony. I could cook us all a meal.'

'Yes.' I was still thinking about Tom Luckham. 'I mean, thanks, that would be lovely.' I didn't feel all that enthusiastic about the invitation. On the other hand, Fay was turning out to be quite good company, so much so that it had even crossed my mind to tell her about the mysterious cassette. I had played the first two tracks, both of which, when you could hear the lyrics above the drum beats, seemed to be about two-timing women who deserved whatever was coming to them. Anonymous communications were never very pleasant, but this time I was certain it had nothing to do with any of my clients. First the car on the Downs, now a slightly menacing cassette. Why was James Luckham so determined to warn me off, and why select a tape where all the songs were dreary diatribes against unfaithful women? Fay was still talking about her landlady, but the sick sensation that had risen in my throat made it difficult to make sense of what she was saying. It wasn't the infidelity James was interested in, but the violence that succeeded it. What were the words on the first track, words that were repeated over and over? *With her life in my hands, they can lock me away.*

The crowd in the pub had thinned out a little, with some of the drinkers moving into a second bar at the back.

'Owen,' Fay was saying, 'the two of you share an apartment?'

'Yes, that's right.'

Fay looked a little cornered, as if she was afraid she had spoken out of turn.

'Sorry,' I said, 'I was just thinking about something. A client I was worried about.'

She nodded sympathetically. 'With a job like yours it must be hard to switch off. People pouring out all their problems, making you feel you're responsible for them, am I right?'

'Yes, it can be like that.' Although we had only just met, perhaps because we had only just met, I found myself wanting to tell her how Owen's trip to Australia had provided something of a welcome breathing space, time to think about the relationship, work out what I really wanted from it. But that would have been unfair on Owen and, besides, I wasn't even sure it was true. When I thought about him, mainly at night when I was finding it difficult to sleep, I could only remember the good part. During the day, various trivial events, like having a bath without having to remove his hairs from my sponge, reminded me of the constant bickering that had preceded his departure to Australia. If you loved someone did it matter if they messed up your bathroom?

'More problems?' said Fay. 'Sorry, only taking a friendly interest. Wouldn't want to step on any toes.'

'You're not,' I said. 'Look, where did you leave your car? My flat's only a short distance away. Why not come back and have some coffee?'

The answering machine was flashing. I rewound the cassette, listened to the usual creaks and squeaks, then jumped slightly when I realized the voice belonged to Howard Fry. *Anna, it's Howard. Look, I know tomorrow's Saturday but Erica Luckham's been on the line. Apparently Sally's remembered something important and you're the only person she'll speak to.*

Chapter Five

My father's train was due at Temple Meads at three-twenty, I had no food in the flat, the carpets needed vacuuming, and Howard expected me to spend Saturday morning at the Luckham house.

Sally answered the door herself, dressed in the same green shorts and panda sweatshirt. The sweatshirt had a spatter of grease spots down the front, the kind that appear if you stand too close to the cooker while having a fry up. I opened my mouth to ask if her throat was better, then decided it would be unfair. If anything she looked healthier, and certainly more cheerful, than the last time I saw her.

'Mummy's got up specially,' she said. 'She wants to talk to you.'

'Good.' But did this mean there *was* no new piece of information, it was just that Mrs Luckham had decided she ought to meet the 'psychiatrist'?

Through the wide-open patio door, I could see a large woman in a blue silk dressing gown standing on the lawn, looking up at the sky. When she heard us approaching she turned slowly, shading her eyes against the sun.

'Mrs Luckham?'

'Yes?' She knew quite well who I was, but she was still going to feign surprise.

'Anna McColl,' I said.

'Yes, of course.' Her speech was a little slurred, as if she were not yet fully awake. 'Sally's told me all about you.' She bent to remove a length of grass that had stuck to the bottom of her bare foot. 'You're a psychologist, whatever that may mean.'

When I drew level I could smell alcohol on her breath. So that was what the cleaner had meant when she'd said her employer was 'indisposed'. How bad a drinking problem did she have? Very bad if it began this early in the morning.

Sally was standing a short distance away, leaning over a large run made out of chicken wire stretched over a wooden frame.

'Guinea pigs,' said Erica Luckham. 'They breed like—well, like guinea pigs, I suppose. My son had the first pair. He's potty about animals. Have you met him? I suppose the policeman told you all about us, not that there's much to tell.' She adjusted the belt of her dressing gown, but not before I had received a full view of her large, sun-tanned breasts. In spite of the fact that she had not bothered to dress she had made an effort with her make-up, concentrating mostly on her eyes, which were surrounded by slightly shaky black lines and two shades of green. Her dark brown hair was flecked with grey and there were deep frown marks between her eyes, but she was still what people call 'a handsome woman'.

'What time is it?' she asked, glancing at her wrist, then realizing she had forgotten to put on her watch. 'Heavens, I've no idea.' Her voice was deep, almost masculine, but perhaps it was the effect of the gin. I had a distinct feeling that, at any moment, she might either burst into tears, or laugh hysterically.

Sally had one of the guinea pigs clasped in her two hands. Its nose protruded between her fingers and it was letting out high-pitched squeaks, but I noticed a calm, relaxed expression on Sally's face that I had never seen before. Smoothing back the animal's fur, she held it to her cheek, rubbing her face against it, then passed it to me.

'Coffee?' said Mrs Luckham. 'Now what was it you wanted to know?'

'No coffee, thanks. Superintendent Fry left a message to say Sally had remembered something and wanted to talk to me. Then perhaps I could have a quick word with you before I leave.'

'With me? In that case I suppose I'd better get some clothes on. Sally, darling, make Dr McColl a cup of coffee, and while you're at it, you can make some for me.'

After she left I put the guinea pig back with its relatives, then asked Sally to tell me all their names.

'That's Matthew.' She indicated a brown and white one, sitting on its own, licking its stomach. 'Then there's Ruth, Joseph, Esther. The one you were holding is called Salome, she's a long-haired Peruvian. Daddy gave her to me.'

'She's beautiful,' I said. 'I'm so sorry about your father, you must miss him a lot.

'He was fifty-one,' she said, almost in the tone that people use, following the death of someone in their eighties or nineties. 'Mummy's only forty-three. Shall

I tell you what I remembered? It's about the car. There was a map on the seat, only not the one of Bristol the lady had in her hand.' She had pulled down her sweatshirt until it reached almost to her knees. When it started to ride up she gave it another tug. 'I think it might have been Manchester.'

'Manchester?'

She nodded uncertainly. 'Something beginning with M.'

'Anything else? Can you remember any more about the driver?'

'No, nothing.' She pulled a leaf off a nearby bush. 'Honestly, if I could I'd tell you. I mean, why wouldn't I?'

'It's all right. I know you're doing your best.'

'Yes, I am. I promise I am.' She had started walking towards a small summer house. I caught up with her just as she pulled open the door and peered inside.

'What does that smell remind you of?' she asked. 'I suppose it's something Daddy used, to preserve the wood, but every time I smell it I think of the house where we used to live.'

'Where was that?'

She looked surprised, as if she expected me to know every detail of the family's past history. 'Near Axbridge', she said, 'only it was different then. Daddy had all these friends who did painting or wrote poetry or played the violin. There was this man who wore a cloak. I think he had a bit of a thing about Mummy, only not really.'

'What was he called?' I could see something lying in the long grass. It would have been a dead bird, or perhaps it was just a curled-up leaf.

'What?' Sally seemed to have forgotten the question. 'Oh, the man in the cloak. Julian, no Jules. Anyway, it doesn't matter. He moved to London and married someone he met on a bus.'

I wondered if her reminiscences were leading up to another revelation about the 'abductor'. It seemed unlikely, but at least she was starting to sound more at ease with me. Howard would have said now was the time to start putting on the pressure, softening her up, then coming out with a shock question that demanded an instant response.

'This is a lovely garden,' I said. 'Does your mother look after it?'

Sally's head jerked round. 'She used to, she loves gardening, but she hasn't been well. James used to mow the lawn, then he saw an advert in a shop window, someone who really needed the work.'

I nodded. I was wondering why James was too busy to cut the grass himself, but presumably he was either in bed—or following people across the Downs in his mustard Capri.

'He's quite nice,' said Sally, and for a moment I was not certain who she was talking about.

'Oh, you mean the gardener.'

Her nose twitched. 'I don't think he's that much older than James, but he's got a moustache and a hairy chest. His name's Col, I suppose it's short for Colin.'

'Do you have any friends who come round to the house?'

'What?' She sighed. 'No, I haven't been at my new school very long. There is one girl, she's called Abigail. I thought we were friends but I think she and Tara are best friends now. Anyway, she thinks I'm a wimp.'

'I wouldn't take any notice,' I said, experiencing a sudden rush of pity as I caught sight of her sad, resigned expression. 'I expect you'll make some friends next term.'

A man was coming through a side gate.

'That's him,' whispered Sally, 'that's Col. I thought he'd be here soon.'

'He works on Saturdays?'

'Yes, I think he's got some other jobs too.' Her eyes were shining. I had never seen her looking so happy.

The man waved, then strolled towards the summer house. 'He's going to make a bigger run for the guinea pigs,' said Sally. 'James said it was a waste of money but Col said he'd do it for nothing.' She stared at me, as if to impress on me that there were some kind people in the world. Then she laughed. 'James is all right really, it's just, well, since Daddy died...' But she never finished the sentence. Col had picked up the dead bird and was carrying it by one wing. A moment later he threw it over the hedge into the next-door garden.

'It was their cat what killed it,' he said, with a grin, 'so I reckon they can have it back.

When we returned to the house Erica was in the drawing room, half inside a cupboard that looked like part of the wall painting, searching through a pile of shoes. Her dressing gown had been exchanged for a white blouse and a pale blue skirt, both of which were slightly too tight.

'D'you have trouble with your feet?' she asked. 'No, I don't suppose you do. When I was a girl the fashions were much prettier, more feminine, but they ruined your toes.' She sat on a low stool, pushing her foot into a navy blue sling-back sandal, like one of the ugly sisters trying on the glass slipper. Except there was nothing ugly about Erica Luckham. Once she had been extremely good-looking; then something had made her drown her sorrows with the help of large quantities of alcohol.

'Tom used to paint me, you know. Oh, I'm talking about twenty years ago when his work meant everything to him. Before he met Neil Hyatt.' Her eyes drifted round the expensively furnished room. 'We used to live in the country. Have you ever lived in the country? The children prefer it there. So did Tom. Well, I thought he did.'

Was she trying to tell me her husband had been depressed? Sufficiently depressed to have...

'Everyone adored Tom,' she said. 'Everyone. You've met people like it, I expect. Larger than life, a wonderful husband and father. Of course, after he and Neil Hyatt found a way of cornering the market... Oh, take no notice, no doubt it was always on the cards.' She gave a kind of snort. 'They say the country would collapse without its voluntary workers.'

It was difficult to follow what she was saying. Who was Neil Hyatt? Someone who organized voluntary work? How had he and Tom Luckham managed to *corner the market?*

'We seem to be moving back to how it was in the old days,' said Erica, stretching out her arms, then letting them drop. 'You disapprove, I expect. For political reasons or because you mistrust amateurs and think all welfare work should be professionalized?'

'No, I don't think...' I began, but she never gave me a chance to answer any of her questions.

'You say you've met James?' She had hauled herself into a chair and was sitting with her head thrown back, patting her neck with her finger tips, as if it was some kind of exercise designed to get rid of a double chin. A pile of glossy magazines lay on the floor near her feet, along with a half-eaten box of Turkish delight. 'James is artistic too,' she said, 'at least I used to think he was. He was out on the tiles last night, haven't seen sight nor sound of him since.'

'He hasn't come home?'

'Oh, it's nothing to worry about, he does it all the time. Crashes out on someone's floor. Crashes out, that's what they call it. He has friends all over Bristol, some of them the most frightful-looking people. You probably think I'm a negligent parent, but quite honestly I've given up.'

'Well, he's eighteen, isn't he? I expect he can take care of himself.'

'Whatever that may mean.' She looked me up and down. 'You haven't any children? You know when I was given your name I pictured someone rather different. Dr McColl sounds terribly grand. You're all doctors, are you, you psychologist people?'

I opened my mouth to explain, but once again she didn't seem to want an answer. She was reaching out, inviting her daughter to come and sit on the arm of her chair. 'Sally had a sudden flash of inspiration, didn't you, darling?'

'It was because of something Abigail once told me,' said Sally. 'You have to close your eyes and pretend you're looking at a black piece of paper. You have to empty your mind, then wait and see what comes into it.'

'And it worked,' I said.

She nodded. 'Oh, I nearly forgot. There was something else. I can remember the colour of the car now too. It was blue, dark blue, and there was a dent in the door.'

'Which door?'

The question seemed to throw her. 'The front one. Yes, it must have been the front one. When the car stopped, before the woman got out.'

'Was it a large dent?'

'No. I'm not sure. Quite large.'

'As if something had bumped into the car?'

'What?' She glanced at her mother, but Erica had closed her eyes and was breathing so heavily I wondered if she had fallen asleep.

'Don't worry,' I told Sally. 'I just wondered if the dent had removed any of the paint.' I smiled at her, but she didn't smile back, and a moment later she was on her way out of the room. She couldn't take any more, or was Howard right, had she invented the 'abduction' as a way of getting her family attention? God knows, with no father and a mother who spent most of her time either in bed or in a drunken stupor, she had good reason to take drastic action. Perhaps she had wanted to impress Abigail, the girl she had hoped was going to be her friend, although if that had been her intention it didn't seem to have worked.

Still with her eyes shut, Erica asked if Sally had been any help.

'Yes, I hope so.' I said. 'Any information about the car, or its driver.'

'Is she making some coffee?' We both paused, listening for sounds coming from the kitchen, but the house was silent.

'James was going to be a marine biologist,' said Erica, 'then staying on at school became a bit of a drag. I expect he'll settle down sooner or later, what do you think?'

This time she seemed to want an answer. 'Yes, I expect so.'

'You know, you can learn a lot from soap operas,' she said, running the last two words together, then repeating them more slowly. 'No doubt you think they're frightfully silly, but at least they keep you in touch with the different generations and the kind of things people do these days.

That's why I know there's nothing much the matter with my son.'

'You and Sally watch the soap operas, do you?' I asked, hoping it was one way they spent some regular time together.

'Sally,' she said vaguely. 'I've been wondering, d'you think it's a mistake to have all your money tied up in property, or will things get back to normal if we all hang on?'

The way she kept changing the subject, it was almost as if she had grown bored with what had happened to Sally, but was quite enjoying having someone else to talk to.

'James,' she said, returning to what seemed to be her favourite subject, 'seems quite happy, just visiting friends, listening to tapes and those CD things. He doesn't play an instrument, never showed the slightest inclination to become a musician, but I expect he'd like to gyrate on a stage. Isn't that what they all want?' She opened the lid of a box of plain chocolates on the coffee table next to her chair, then realized the box was empty and dropped it into a leather waste-paper bin.

Is James the kind of boy who would send someone a threatening cassette? It was hardly a question I could put to his mother.

'Sally seems to be feeling a little better,' I said. 'Perhaps in a day or two, she'll feel confident enough to go out, see some friends.'

'What friends?' Erica stood up, smoothing her skirt over her hips. 'Best to just forget all about it, wouldn't you say, like falling off a horse and climbing straight back on again.'

'She seems quite friendly with the man who mows your lawn.'

'What about him?' She sounded irritated, as if she thought I had stirred up quite enough trouble for one day. 'James got his name off some advert at the newsagent. Seems efficient enough, reasonably hard-working. You know, you want to take what Sally tells you with a pinch of salt. She spends too much time on her own, and adamantly refuses to join the Guides or whatever girls her age do these days.'

'You think she's lonely?'

'Lonely? I was just explaining how she prefers her own company.' She pointed to a small picture on the wall that I had failed to notice before. 'One of Tom's landscapes, painted when he was very young, only just out of art school. What d'you think?'

I stood up to study it more closely. 'It's Dorset, isn't it?'

'Oh, you know that area.' She seemed pleased. 'Later, he moved on to a more abstract phase, but he never abandoned his watercolours altogether, not until he met Neil Hyatt. Flash Harry, I called him. No aesthetic feeling whatsoever, but you couldn't fault his business sense. Had Tom churning out prints by the dozen. Of course it was all very lucrative.'

'You needed the money?'

She pressed her finger against her upper lip, as if to prevent a sneeze. 'I suppose so. Who knows? We'd never been badly off, not with the investments Tom made, but perhaps they'd lost some of their value, or perhaps...' She stood up and joined me near the small watercolour. 'You know Stephen Bryce, don't you? Poor Ros, when I think what happened I could spit.'

Did she mean Stephen's decision to leave the parish, or was she talking about something else? I never had the chance to find out. By the time she had finished the sentence she was halfway through the patio door and there was no question of my being invited to accompany her into the garden.

When I left, Sally was standing on the pavement, close to where I had left my car.

'All right?' I asked, but there was no reply and when I looked at her more closely I could see that she was clenching and unclenching her jaw. 'Look, don't worry, no one expects miracles. It's good you've remembered as much as you have.'

She raised her head and stared into the distance, gazing at the trees at the top of the Avon Gorge. 'Will I have to go to court?'

'Only if they catch the person who—'

'But they won't, will they?'

'Is that what you're afraid of?' I meant the court, but she took it to mean she was frightened her attacker might come back for her.

'I haven't been out on my own since it happened. Abigail phoned. She's my friend from school, well, sort of. She wants me to go round, to tell her what happened, only her father's away and her mother's lost her licence.'

'Couldn't your mother take you?' Was she angling for a lift? If it wasn't too far

I probably had time. But who would bring her home?

'No, it's all right, I'll ask James, only, the thing is, no one knows where he is.'

'I expect he'll be back soon.'

'Yes.' Her eyes had a far-away look and when she spoke again her voice was so quiet I had to read her lips. 'Will you be coming again?'

She looked so worried, but I was not sure if it was because she thought she might be asked more questions, or because she was afraid it was my last visit.

'D'you want me to come back?'

Her head moved. It could have been a nod. 'Do *you* think Daddy was murdered?' Then, without waiting for an answer, she ran back through the gate, across a patch of rough grass and disappeared round the side of the house.

Bristol Temple Meads. I could see my father through the swing doors. He was wearing his usual dark grey trousers, but the jacket was new, and so were the thick-soled shoes. He glanced at his watch, then up at the arrivals board.

'Dad?'

He turned quickly, picking up his small

leather suitcase, then putting it down again to give me a slightly awkward hug. 'You're out of breath.'

'I had trouble finding a parking space, then I saw all the people coming out and guessed you'd arrived early.'

Now that the greetings were over we were struggling to think of things to say to each other. My father was my one remaining parent, and the hours of time we would have to spend together—although, for heaven's sake, he was only staying one night—stretched ahead like an onerous job of work. He looked tired, a little older than the last time, but perhaps not. The photo in my bedroom—both my parents standing under a tree in Kew Gardens—had been taken six years ago. That image of my mother was fixed for all time—cheerful, smiling, holding back her hair against the wind—but my father could live another twenty years, become crippled with arthritis. Why had I always assumed he would die first? And how, after all this time, could I still feel so angry that it had been the other way round?

'Had a good journey?' I asked, negotiating the car through the narrow exit, then accelerating as the lights turned green and the traffic on Temple Gate gave way to the stream of cars leaving the station.

'Tiring,' said my father. 'Crossing London's become something of a nightmare. The underground's far more crowded than it used to be. I was accosted by a group of foreign students, Dutch I think they were, going the wrong way round the Circle Line. D'you visit London much?'

'Not that often.' His question had felt like a reproach. *If you can go up to London why can't you continue your journey and come down to Kent for the weekend?* But I was being oversensitive. He was only making conversation, trying to ease the tension.

As we passed the supermarket in Coronation Road he began telling me how he had started attending an evening class in oriental cooking.

'Really?' When my mother was alive his one contribution to the day-to-day running of the house had been to wash up on Christmas Day.

'The presentation of the food is very important,' he said, looking over his shoulder to check that his suitcase was on the back seat. 'In the sense that if it looks unappetizing, it probably won't taste that good either.'

'No, I can see that.' So even my cooking was going to be under scrutiny. Lucky I had booked us a table in a French restaurant off Cotham Hill—close to where Geena Robson had been abducted.

He was craning his neck to catch a glimpse of the river. 'Funnily enough, there are more men than women in the class. Of course, most of them are a good deal younger than I am. One of them's a research assistant at Kent University, and there's an interesting chap who worked for years in Kenya, or was it Uganda?'

We had reached the place where the road curves sharply, then straightens out again as it approaches the underpass. 'Sounds like good fun,' I said, trying to concentrate on three things at once: my father's evening class, the truck in front of me that appeared to have no brake lights, and the figure on the pavement, crouching down to talk to a baby in a buggy. The baby's mother came out of the garage shop and joined them. She looked about eighteen or nineteen. She was wearing black shorts and a white bikini top. Her ash-blonde hair was so short it gave the impression her head had been shaved, then the hair had been allowed to grow back until it reached about a quarter of an inch. When the traffic started moving again I glanced in the driving mirror and saw them crossing to the opposite side of the road. The man was pushing the buggy and the girl was hanging on to his arm, laughing, with her white plastic bag of shopping held up high out of his reach. The man was James Luckham.

Chapter Six

Sunday morning, and my father had decided to attend Family Communion. Since he had selected Stephen Bryce's old church, part of me had been tempted to accompany him, but he would have thought I was humouring him and that would have spoiled things between us.

The previous evening had turned out better than I expected. During dinner, at the French restaurant, specially selected because I knew my father would fall for *le patron's* exaggerated charm, I had told him about the Luckham family and my latest phone call from Howard Fry and how enraged I had been.

'The girl remembered that the car had a dent in the passenger door,' I said. 'Apparently this could be important. A man reported seeing someone answering the description of the missing schoolgirl, and said that the car she was in had quite a few scratches and bumps. Anyway, despite the fact that it was me who found out

95

about the dent, Howard started accusing me of giving the girl psychotherapy when all he wanted was a description of the person who had tried to abduct her.'

'Yes, I see.' My father was trying to appreciate my disgust.

'The thing is,' I explained, 'if I put any more pressure on her she'll just clam up and refuse to talk to me at all.'

'Yes. Tricky.' He was studying the menu and, just for a moment, his absorbed expression reminded me of Owen. 'But I suppose it must be a matter of some urgency to obtain an accurate description of who abducted the first girl.'

So he was going to take Howard's side.

'Presumed dead, is she?' he asked. 'This Howard Fry chap, you've known him quite a time as I recall.'

I nodded, then changed the subject and started talking about Owen and how he had sent me a postcard with a picture of some faerie penguins walking up the beach at dusk.

The sudden switch of subject was not lost on my father. 'Missing him, are you?' he said. 'Or is it giving you a bit of a break?'

'Why d'you say that, Dad?'

'Oh, no reason. You tell me so little about your affairs of the heart I have to pick up clues here and there and draw my own conclusions. Now, red or white? I prefer white, myself, but I suppose you're meant to drink red with boeuf en croûte.'

The rest of the evening had gone well. My father told me how he had joined some kind of club and was starting to go out more, although he played down the enjoyment he derived from making new friends, glancing at me every so often in case I felt he was being disloyal to my mother.

'I'm glad,' I said, wondering if he was leading up to telling me he had formed a close relationship with someone. 'I used to worry about the amount of time you spent on your own.'

'The lonely widower.' He adjusted the knot in his tie. 'Apparently we're quite in demand. Oh, don't worry, I've no plans on that front. You know me, far too rigid to adjust to any change to my nice, orderly way of life.'

In the morning he had been up early, preparing for the ten forty-five service. We had walked together, as far as

Queen's Road, then parted company, waving goodbye as he turned the corner, reassuring each other that we would meet up again around twelve...

It was nearly half past. I could see him coming down the road, walking briskly, and as straight-backed as ever, and as I watched, he turned to look at the floating harbour, shading his eyes with his hand, and the sun caught the bald spot on the back of his head. He had a new suit, dark grey, with a thin chalk stripe, that made him look even slimmer. Had he lost weight? If some incurable illness had been diagnosed would he tell me, or keep up a pretence that everything was fine, right up to the last possible moment? For a time I had thought he was going to join my brother in Australia, but when I asked him he'd looked astonished and insisted it was the last thing he intended to do. Was that the moment I should have invited him to live with me? He was still only sixty-eight, but what would happen in five or ten years' time?

He was standing on the kerb, waiting for the cars to pass, tapping his foot impatiently, but looking rather pleased with life. I worried too much. The new clothes were a good sign. In spite of what he had said about being too old to adjust to change, I had a feeling some determined woman, a widow or divorcee, would be able to talk him round. A moment later he crossed over and disappeared from view, and I listened as he climbed the outside steps and knocked discreetly on the door to my flat.

'Good service?' I followed him into the living room and offered him the dry sherry, which I knew he would first turn down, then change his mind and accept.

'Church was surprisingly full,' he said. 'Apparently the vicar left a few months back, some rift with the bishop. They had a locum today, elderly chap come out of retirement to fill in for a month or two. Parish seems divided about what happened, with some believing the vicar had a right to his opinions, even though they were at odds with the teachings of the Church, and the rest convinced he did the right thing to resign.'

'Stephen Bryce,' I said.

'Oh, you know him.'

'No, not really. It was in the papers for a week or two.'

He looked at me suspiciously. 'Really? I

wouldn't have thought the general public would have been greatly interested, but I suppose the gutter press hinted at some impropriety, tried to make out the book was just a cover story.'

'Yes, I expect so, but as far as I can remember there wasn't a shred of evidence.'

I was wondering if someone in the congregation had said something. Perhaps my father had heard whispering, rumours, although, since it was three months since Bryce's resignation, this seemed unlikely.

'They give you a cup of coffee these days.' He accepted his sherry, took a small sip, then placed the glass on the mantelpiece, next to the china cat he had given me for my tenth birthday. 'After the service, in the parish hall, that's why I was late back. All very friendly, but none of that dreadful kissing and hugging, thank the Lord. Quite a coincidence, I met two sisters who used to live in Kent, only a mile or so from the house. And some people called Young. He runs a shop and the wife, I think she said she used to be a health visitor or something. Had a tragedy in the family. Daughter died while she was still at school.'

'How awful.' It seemed a little odd that they had chosen such a sensitive subject, when talking to a total strange, but perhaps they had taken an instant liking to my father. People sometimes did.

'Reason they mentioned it, this Bryce chap was a great help to them at the time. Mr Young couldn't praise him enough, seemed outraged at the bishop's decision.'

'I thought it was by mutual agreement—Stephen Bryce leaving the Church.'

He stared at me, running his finger round the rim of his glass. 'That wasn't the impression I got, Anna. You may be right; I've a feeling you know more about the case than you're letting on, but the people I spoke to—the ones who had wanted Bryce to stay—seemed to feel he'd been treated rather badly.'

He caught the early evening train back to London. During the afternoon, while we were walking on the Downs, I had tried to persuade him to stay another night, then discovered he had arranged to see his brother in Hatfield, returning home on Tuesday. His brief visit had been a success, and I should have been feeling pleased, relieved, but for some reason I had no wish to return to my empty flat.

When I reached the flyover I made a split-second decision and swung left towards the Portway. Either I would take a long roundabout route home, collecting my thoughts as I drove, or I would call in on Chris and Bruce. The traffic was thick, people returning from a day in the sun, and I had at least ten minutes to make up my mind, but even before I had passed the turning to the zoo I realized that what I needed was some noisy, undemanding company. Apart from my colleagues at work, Chris was the person I had known the longest since moving to Bristol, and unless she and Bruce were in the middle of one of their big rows, it was the kind of household where you always felt welcome. Chris would be talking her head off and the children—four of them now—would be rushing in and out, quarrelling and complaining. My presence would mean Bruce was detailed to put them all to bed, but he never seemed to mind—why should he, they were his children after all—and if he did object to the way Chris handed out instructions, he would never give away his true feelings, not in front of me.

Every light had been turned on, at least

at the front of the house. Jack answered the door, holding an improvised machete that he waved above his head as he preceded me into the kitchen.

Chris had heard my voice. She was crouched by a low cupboard, searching for something, pulling out piles of old supermarket bags. 'About time!' she screeched, without looking round. 'We haven't seen you for an age and, as you can see, you've dropped in at a really good moment, we're all having such fun.' She straightened up and nodded in the direction of the machete. 'Well, what d'you expect in a house where toy guns are banned? Bruce is upstairs helping Rosie to bath Fraser, and Barnaby and Jack are having a lovely game of guerrilla warfare.' Her face was contorted in mock agony. 'God, once you've given birth your back's never the same again.'

'I should think it's the pregnancy, isn't it, rather than the actual giving birth.'

She picked up a newspaper and threatened to swipe me across the head. 'Why d'you have to be so bloody literal? Of course it's the pregnancy. Fatso was nine and a half pounds. Would you like to drag round nine and a half pounds for—' She broke off in mid-sentence. 'What's the matter? You only come round if you're in a bad way. No, don't deny it.'

'I've just seen my father off at Temple Meads.'

'He was here for the weekend?'

'Just one night. Anyway, I'm fine and I'm not expecting anything to eat or drink, just give me something useful to do.'

I expected her to make a sarcastic remark. Instead, she looked at her watch, did some mental arithmetic, and announced that in precisely ten minutes' time Barnaby and Fraser would be in bed, the other two would be watching telly, and the three of us—if Bruce insisted on joining in—could sit in the kitchen and drink a bottle of fairly disgusting wine.

In spite of the draining board being covered in unwashed pans and baking trays, and the newspaper scattered over the floor, Chris seemed more organized than usual. Presumably with four kids you had to stick to a fairly strict routine, or maybe Bruce had got tough with her, for once, and come to some agreement about who did what. An hour later, when the two youngest were tucked up in bed and I had been up and down stairs several times with a variety of bears, rabbits and books, the painful feelings my father's departure had elicited were starting to recede.

'Your dad's retired, hasn't he?' said Bruce. 'Lucky bastard, I've another thirty-one years, unless they bring down the retirement age for men.'

'God, you're boring.' Chris had found three smeary glasses and was pouring out the wine. Her hair hung in damp strands and she had dark smudges under her eyes. 'How was your father, Anna?' she asked. 'You should have him to live with you. No, I mean buy a bigger place, with an annexe or something.'

'He went to church this morning,' I said, 'that one where the vicar had to give up his job.'

'Really?' Chris put her elbows on the table and leaned forward, hoping for a large helping of scurrilous gossip. 'What did he do, touch up choirboys in the vestry?'

'No, nothing like that,' I began, but Bruce interrupted me.

'You remember, it was in the paper, even made the nationals. *The vicar who doesn't believe in God.* A bloke at work has a friend who's a lay reader, not at that church, on the other side of the city, but apparently there was more to the story than the press let out. Don't ask me how the powers that be managed to hush it up.'

'You never told me,' Chris was indignant. 'He never tells me anything interesting, Anna, just endless stuff about the housing department and—'

'Well, it wasn't particularly interesting.' Bruce looked tired, but perhaps no more than usual. 'Just the same old thing, mucking about with female parishioners. Anyway, it could be a pack of lies, you know how these rumours take on a life of their own.'

'What did this friend say exactly?' It was impossible to hide my curiosity.

'You see,' said Chris, tipping the remains of the wine into her glass, then lifting the bottle up to the light and pulling a face. 'You love gossip just as much as I do. You pretend to be so serious, so professional, but really—'

'No, I don't.'

'Oh, come on.' She reached across the table and gave me a push. 'Only joking. Off you go, Bruce, that shop on the corner's started selling booze, go and buy another bottle.'

Bruce stood up slowly, taking his wallet from an inside pocket and inspecting the contents. 'I'll tell you, Anna, if you want to know more about Stephen Bryce you should talk to some of his old parishioners. Apparently some born again bloke, an actor, artist or something, joined the congregation a year or two back and persuaded Bryce to take a more evangelical approach.'

'How d'you mean? New style services? Pop music to get in some younger people? My father never mentioned anything like that.'

'No, well according to this bloke I met, the leading light, new convert, whatever you want to call him, went walking on the Mendips last winter and had some kind of accident.'

'Fatal?' Chris's voice was breathless with excitement.

Bruce yawned. 'After that, I suppose things returned to normal. Maybe it had something to do with Bryce leaving the parish.'

'What did?' I asked.

Bruce shrugged. 'Maybe the squalid stories are the kind people always spread if someone in a position of moral authority hands in his resignation. Even better if it's a bishop, and as for a High Court Judge!'

The following day I had lunch with Nick. We sat in our usual corner of our usual haunt and I prepared for his inevitable complaints about the way Heather and I seemed to have it in for Dawn Rivers. But he had something else on his mind. He was wearing new clothes: grey cotton trousers and a black tracksuit top over a gleaming white T-shirt. His hair was different too, shorter, and with something on it that made it glisten slightly, and from the way his face kept breaking into a grin I had a feeling he was going to behave uncharacteristically and let me in on what was going on in his life. Perhaps the Jake he mentioned now and again, but only in passing, had moved in with him. Perhaps he had met someone new.

Then, all at once, his expression became serious. 'This work you're doing for the CID,' he said, 'you're not overdoing things, are you? How much of your time is it taking up?'

'It's not interfering with my other clients,' I said defensively.

'No, I wasn't suggesting it was, but if

Howard Fry keeps putting pressure on you to get more out of the Luckham girl... How much does he really know about how we work? There's so much rubbish talked these days, as if psychology was on a par with chemistry and physics, although we know it's more of an art.'

'Not everyone would agree with that, Nick.'

'Oh, come on, all the research shows it's the relationship between psychologist and client that counts, not the appliance of science. Anyway, from what you were telling me about the Luckhams, Fry seems to expect miracles.'

I glanced round, then suggested Nick keep his voice down. It was unlikely that anyone who knew the Luckham family would be sitting in the White Hart, but Sally's attempted abduction had made the local paper so the name might be familiar.

'I can handle Howard,' I said.

Nick raised his eyebrows. 'Actually I've never been too sure about you and Fry. No, don't say anything, apart from telling me to mind my own business.'

'I had a letter from Owen,' I said. 'It's winter in Melbourne. I never thought it got that cold in Australia but apparently the fountain in the centre of the city has frozen over. Of course, being Owen, he hadn't even packed his coat.'

'How long is he there for?'

'Until the end of September. He had a few invitations to stay with people but he's rented a place, prefers it that way.'

'Missing him?'

'Of course.'

Nick gave me a funny look. 'He's good for you, you know.'

'So people keep telling me. Now, what's all this about?' I pointed at the new clothes and trendy hairstyle.

'You know me, Anna, like to keep up standards. No, seriously, with the work we do, I think it's important to look on top of things, make sure the clients don't start reversing roles.'

'Meaning what?'

'Meaning nothing. Oh, for goodness sake, I'm talking about myself, not you. Last week this woman I've been seeing, seventy if she's a day, brought me a present, a sweater she'd knitted and two pairs of socks.'

I laughed. 'Oh, come on, everyone has clients like that. Miss Simpson, was it, the one who has panic attacks in the library? You're the little boy she never had. Anyway, it sounds as if she's feeling a whole lot better.'

Nick stood up to buy more drinks, but I indicated it was my turn. 'What d'you want, another half?

'No, one's my limit or I doze off during the afternoon. Just an orange juice, thanks.'

I reached down to pick up my bag but it had slipped under the chair, or so I thought. It wasn't on the spare seat either, or across Nick's side. I started to panic.

'My bag's gone.'

'It can't have.' Nick had his head under the table. 'Sure you brought it with you? You could've just put your purse—'

'No, I never leave it at the office.' I stood up and looked round wildly, trying to remember who had been sitting near us, or anyone who had walked past. It was no good. I had been too busy thinking about Nick to take in what was happening round about me.

'That old bloke, who always wears a hat, was sitting over there,' said Nick, indicating a wooden bench a few yards away.

'Harold? He'd never do a thing like that.

Who else was here? Anyone you've never seen before?'

'Don't think so. Couple of middle-aged women, but they didn't come close enough to steal a bag. Oh, there was one person. A woman.'

'What did she look like?' My heart had started to race.

'No idea, I'm afraid. She had her head turned away so I never saw her face. Brown hair, I think, tied back, and it looked exceptionally shiny, like in a shampoo ad, although real hair hardly ever looks that way.'

'You're sure it was tied back?'

'Yes, I think so. Oh, and glasses, dark ones, like a washed-up actress pretending to hide from all her fans. She was wearing high heels, I'm certain about that, and she seemed to be having difficulty keeping her balance. She bent down and I thought her foot must have slipped out of her shoe. Oh God, you don't think...'

Chapter Seven

Howard Fry was unavailable. Not that he was likely to have much interest in the loss of my bag but Nick's description of the thief was another matter. When I started to explain to the desk sergeant, a gloomy-looking man I had never come across before, he suggested I talk to DS Whittle. 'If you'd like to wait in here, love, I'll see if he's free.'

The interview room was stuffy and smelled of disinfectant, and when Graham Whittle arrived the first thing he did was to fling open a window.

'Right, Anna, how can I help? Howard's in a meeting but I'm sure you can talk to him later. Of course, if it's urgent...'

'It's not.' I told him what had happened and he tactfully resisted the temptation to point out that I had provided even less in the way of a useful description than Sally Luckham had been able to do.

'I don't even remember seeing the

woman,' I said, 'but Nick thought she was wearing dark glasses and had shiny brown hair.'

'So you put two and two together and made... Sorry, you're thinking it could be the same person that tried to snatch the Luckham girl. Well, I suppose it's a possibility.' I could tell he was just being polite. 'But surely there must be thousands of women in Bristol with shiny brown hair, whatever that may mean. Anyway, you've been in touch with the bank, I hope, about your credit cards? How much cash was there?'

'Oh, only six or seven pounds.'

'But it's a nasty experience,' he said. 'Address book? Letters?'

'Lottery ticket,' I said. 'I only buy one once in a blue moon. I've tried to forget the numbers—just in case they come up this week—but no matter how hard I try they're imprinted on my brain.'

'Worked out a special system, have you, or do you use people's birthdays? They say you shouldn't do that, too many people pick the lower numbers. Any other valuables?'

I shook my head. 'Library card, video rental membership, couple of first class stamps. Is there any more news about the missing girl?'

Graham was making a few notes. He looked up, trying to remember something. 'What did Sally Luckham say about the driver's hair?'

'Brown. Tied back. Glossy.'

He nodded. 'Geena Robson's mother received another silent phone call, but Howard thinks it's unlikely to have much significance. Phone calls, anonymous letters, it's always the same with a case like this. If people understood how it interfered with the real evidence, not that there is any real evidence, just reports from various parts of the British Isles, people claiming to have spotted a girl answering Geena's description. Nothing we've followed up has come to anything.'

'Mrs Robson lives alone, doesn't she?'

'Yes, that's right. Husband moved in with another woman two years ago, but we've checked and double-checked that angle.'

He pushed aside his notebook, as if to indicate he was changing from a policeman into a friend.

'Howard said anything recently? I know his wife's moved to Scotland. Must be hard for him to see the boy.'

'You'll know more about it than I do then, Graham. Why the interest?'

'Oh, I just wondered... He's been a bit ratty just recently.'

'He's always ratty.'

Graham grinned. 'Yes, but the rattiness usually comes and goes. During the last month or so it's become a permanent fixture.'

'He accused me of giving Sally Luckham some kind of psychological treatment when what was wanted were a few hard facts.'

'Yes, but he rates you, Anna. I heard him talking about you, only last week, on the phone to the Assistant Chief Constable.'

'You mean he has a passing interest in psychological techniques.'

'Oh, don't be like that. With Howard it's a question of reading between the lines. The hidden agenda—isn't that what they call it?'

'You tell me, Graham, you know him far better than I do.'

'Oh, I wouldn't say that, no, I definitely wouldn't say that.' And he was off on a familiar story about the first time he and Howard Fry had met, and how Howard had confused him with someone who had been locked up in the cells the previous week.

When the story finally came to an end he asked about the uniformed constable he had referred to me about a month ago.

'No details, Anna, just wondered if he got to you all right. He hasn't said anything about an appointment.'

He was talking about one of his colleagues, a young PC who had witnessed a nasty pile-up on the motorway and was having recurrent nightmares. Graham had suggested he get in touch with the Psychology Service and the man had arrived for his first appointment, convinced I possessed some miraculous technique and that one forty minute session would rid him of his bad dreams for ever. Needless to say, the road traffic accident had turned out to be the least of his problems.

'I've seen him once,' I said, 'but I've a feeling he was afraid it might be held against him, seeing a psychologist. Go down on his record, making him appear unstable.'

'We're not like that.' Graham looked outraged. 'I'll have a word, shall I?'

'No, don't do that. I think I managed to convince him there wouldn't be a problem.

As a matter of fact I'm seeing him again later in the day.'

'Good. Now, to return to your bag. We've got a description so it's possible the bag itself may be handed in, although it's unlikely the cash and cards will still be there.'

'I'm not all that bothered about it,' I lied. 'Just tell Howard about the woman with brown hair and dark glasses.'

'It's August. Plenty of people wear sunglasses.'

'In the pub?'

We were walking down the corridor. A door squeaked open, and Graham seemed to know who would be coming out. 'You can tell him yourself,' he whispered, 'and now's your chance to meet Ritsema. I know Howard's been looking forward to introducing him.'

DCI Ritsema turned out to be rather different from what I was expecting. Broadly built with a small moustache and very little hair, he looked more like a kindly uncle than a bullying cop. Graham explained about the bag and, while Howard gave the impression he was barely listening, Ritsema seemed surprisingly keen to talk to me.

His office was on the first floor. Compared with Howard's obsessionally tidy room it was a mess. Folders and files lay in piles on the floor and the desk was covered with more papers and the remains of a cheese and pickle sandwich.

'My daughters,' he said, picking up a large photograph that had fallen on its face. 'Fifteen and thirteen, just the age they think they've the right do whatever they like. Reckon that's why the Geena Robson case has got to me a bit.'

'Yes, I can understand that.'

'You can?' I wondered if he was being sarcastic, but his expression was serious. 'Expect Howard told you how I mishandled the interview with Sally Luckham.'

'She's not the easiest of people,' I said, hoping it would help the two of us to get off to a good start. 'I mean, it's not that easy persuading her to talk.'

'You can say that again.' He rubbed his forehead with the palm of his hand and I wondered if he had a headache. 'Perhaps she's told us everything she saw. This description of the car—think it rings true, or has she started inventing things, just to get us off her back?'

'I'm not sure, but I think it's worth

119

talking to her again, if only to establish how consistent her story is.'

He stood up and walked towards the window. When he turned round he had his arms folded and I could see how Sally might have been intimidated by him. Most of the muscles in his face remained very still when he talked, but at the end of each sentence he had a way of moving his mouth, almost as if he was sucking a boiled sweet.

'Yes, keep trying,' he said. 'Joan Robson seems to have virtually given up hope. I suppose because she's so certain her daughter wasn't the type to just run off without leaving a message or getting in touch later on, but if it was one of mine... You think you know your own kids, but once they're teenagers they start to clam up, never tell you a bloody thing.'

'They need some privacy, want to assert their independence.'

'Oh, I know the psychology of it,' he said gloomily. 'Doesn't make us parents feel any better though, does it? S'pose you think it should.'

As it turned out my policeman client was late. Perhaps he had lost his nerve and decided one visit was enough. The waiting room was empty, apart from Heather, tidying up the old copies of *Woman* and *Woman's Own* that were passed on to her by a neighbour.

'Your client's in the loo,' she said.

'Oh, that's where he is.'

'He? Oh, heavens, Anna, your policeman changed to Wednesday so I booked in someone new. Didn't I tell you?'

'It doesn't matter, but who is it? Who made the referral?'

'Oh, that's easy, she referred herself. She said you'd know who she was so I assumed you must have talked to her before. Her name's Ros Bryce.'

I could hear footsteps in the passage and when I put my head round the door a woman was standing in the entrance hall, staring at her feet.

'Mrs Bryce?'

'I've come to see Dr McColl.' She made it sound like a dreaded appointment with her dentist.

'I'm Anna McColl,' I said, holding out my hand, 'if you'd like to come upstairs?' With my foot on the first step, I turned to smile at her but she was busy adjusting her shoulder bag, pulling the strap closer to her neck, then smoothing the lapel of her jacket.

Once inside my room she started talking even before she sat down. 'I've no idea why I'm here or what I'm supposed to say. Stephen's always been interested in psychology, psychotherapy, all that kind of thing, but I think Freud just succeeded in making life more complicated. *Civilisation and its Discontents:* Have you read it? Yes, of course you have.'

So she read Freud. Suddenly, instead of being a sceptical, rather aggressive woman, who had come to prove I was no use to her, she turned into someone of more than average interest.

'What was it that decided you to make an appointment?' I asked.

'Oh, I did it to get Stephen off my back. For some obscure reason he seems to think I'm incapable of sorting out my own life. Coming here was part of the bargain. Now he's agreed to leave me in peace.'

She knew what she was saying was illogical. There was no need for her to come and see me. She could simply have told Stephen she no longer wished to have anything to do with him.

I pulled out a chair, but she continued

to stand. 'In due course, I suppose there'll be a legal separation,' she said, 'and, if Stephen wants it, a divorce.' Snapping open her bag she reached inside and retrieved two rather grimly-looking tablets. 'Would you like some water?'

'No, thank you, I don't need water. I've been getting bad headaches, you'll say it's psychosomatic, nervous tension, but it could just as well be my reading glasses. I should've had my eyes re-tested months ago.'

She was older than her husband, or perhaps it was her rather old-fashioned clothes that made her seem older. Her wiry brown hair came to just below her ears and I guessed, although I could have been quite wrong, that she had worn it in the same style most of her adult life. She sat down at last, smoothed her skirt over her knees, then adjusted her belt and checked that all the buttons were done up on her light blue school-style blouse. Everything about her was extremely neat—even, I suspected, the inside of her handbag. The tissue she took out had been folded twice. She placed it on her knees, then changed her mind and pushed it up her sleeve.

123

'How much has Stephen told you?' she asked. 'No point in boring you, going over the same ground all over again. We've been married eleven years. I'm two years older, but people tend to think the age difference is greater. We met at Glastonbury, on a weekend retreat. We've no children, so when we moved out of the vicarage there was no great organizational problem, apart from what to do with the furniture.'

'Even so, it must have been difficult for you when your husband decided to give up his job.'

She said nothing, just nodded vaguely and focused her gaze on one of the pictures on the wall. Her eyes were slightly red-rimmed, but it could have been due to an allergy rather than the result of crying. On the other hand, perhaps it was easier to break down while she was driving along in the car, rather than in someone else's home.

'Stephen's an intellectual,' she said at last, 'interested in ideas and complicated theological debates. I suppose I'm more unquestioning. A simple faith, isn't that what they call it?'

First impressions made this statement

difficult to believe. It was as if she was inviting me to treat her the way she felt she had been treated by everyone for years: the model vicar's wife who could be relied on to support her husband and carry out whatever duties were required, while Stephen wrote his books and sermons and played the role of a spiritual leader. I wanted to ask her about the events leading up to Stephen's resignation. I had looked up accounts of the story in the national press and discovered the usual veiled hints that some personal indiscretion could have been involved and it was not just a question of the bishop's disapproval of his book, but not a single investigative journalist had managed to come up with any specific accusation.

'If I were you,' I said cautiously, ' I think I might feel quite angry.'

She laughed. 'Oh, don't worry, I am. You don't have to tiptoe round my feelings. I'm forty, nearly forty-one. In a manner of speaking my whole life's been devoted to the Church, now I'm...' She held up her hand. 'No, don't try and reassure. I can see you're an intelligent woman, and if we're going to get on we must talk in equal terms.'

'Yes, of course.'

'Tom Luckham,' she said suddenly. 'Stephen said you'd met the family. He was an amazing person, I doubt if I've met anyone with so much energy.'

'So I keep hearing.'

Her head shot up. 'Yes, well, I'm sure you would.' She stretched out a foot to retrieve the flat brown shoe that had slipped off one of her feet. 'Stephen thinks I blamed Tom for his decision to leave the Church, but that's nonsense.'

I waited for her to go on, but she was staring at me, willing me to ask questions.

'I believe you're staying with a friend at present, near Bath.'

'Not a friend exactly. What constitutes a friend? They say someone's only a real friend when you've fallen out with her, then made it up. Livvy and I have known each other for several years but I'd never confide in her, it's not that sort of a friendship, and in any case she's quite enough problems of her own.'

'Yes, I see.' I cut her short, afraid she might be planning to spend the rest of the time talking about her friend, just as Stephen Bryce had talked about *her*. 'It

126

can't be easy for you, not being in your own home.'

'No, it's not easy, but why should everything be easy?' She was glaring at me, then suddenly she relented and managed a weak smile. 'If I'm honest, I suppose I went to stay with Livvy precisely because of her problems. It was infinitely preferable to thinking about mine. Well, that's how you'd see it, isn't it? Of course, Livvy adored Tom. She talks about him all the time.'

'Did Mr Luckham know about Stephen's book? I mean, had he read it?'

She frowned. 'Yes, I suppose so, they spent enough time together. As different as chalk from cheese, but that's no bad thing from the point of view of the parishioners.'

'I believe Tom Luckham was very active in the parish.' I remembered what Bruce had said, but wanted Ros to think I knew nothing, apart from what Stephen had told me.

'Like all new converts, Tom was something of an idealist, but he was no fool. He believed that unless you took the teaching of the Bible very seriously indeed you were heading for the slippery slope.' Her hands were clasped together so tightly that the

127

knuckles showed white. She became aware of where I was looking and let them drop to her lap. 'I'm talking about the New Testament, of course. Tom was no fundamentalist, going on about the Garden of Eden, but he liked to quote from St Matthew, chapter five, verse forty-four: "Let your light so shine before men, that they may see your good works, and glorify your Father which is in heaven." If he'd had his way I believe he'd have given up all his material possessions and lived a simple life. Like Jesus, I suppose.'

A shudder ran through her body and she adjusted her position on her chair, folded her hands on her lap, and sat up very straight. 'Now, what are you supposed to do for me? I have a feeling the Job Centre might've been more appropriate. One ex-vicar's wife, unemployed, with no dependents, the minimum of qualifications and no prospects whatsoever.'

I had promised my father I would try and find him a projector for his wildlife slides, which were not the usual 35mm variety but needed a special medium-format model. Flicking through the photography section in one of the free-ad newspapers I became guiltily aware of the person behind the counter and decided I had better buy a copy.

The woman had a streaming cold and as she took the money, she turned her head, overcome by a fit of coughing.

'You ought to be in bed,' I said.

'Who with?' She pressed a wad of tissues to her mouth, and at the same moment a voice behind me spoke my name.

Turning round sharply I found myself face to face with James Luckham.

'Just been visiting a friend,' he said, unconvincingly.

'How did you know where I worked?'

He opened his mouth to say bumping into me had been pure coincidence, then changed his mind. 'Will you be seeing my sister again?'

'It depends.'

'On what?' He had a tiny mole on his cheek bone, and another just below his lower lip. Close to, he was just as good looking as I remembered, but they were the kind of looks that are better on a young boy than an older man. Smooth skin, turned up nose, wide apart eyes. I wondered if his father had had a similar appearance, if part of Tom Luckham's appeal had been animal magnetism rather than the fact he was such a wonderfully selfless person.

'Depends on what?' James repeated.

'Whether Sally remembers anything new. Whether the police gain additional information about the other case and need the answer to a particular question.'

We had left the newsagent's and were standing outside a bakery, with its window full of pink meringues with faces, and those cakes in the shape of pyramids, covered in jam and slivers of coconut.

James leaned against the glass. 'She's only a kid,' he said, 'don't you think she's been through enough?'

I wasn't sure if he meant the incident with the car, or whether he was referring to his father's death as well.

'That's why I was asked to talk to her,' I said. 'The police thought I might be less intimidating.'

'I thought they had policewomen trained for that kind of thing. Psychologists usually seem to make a balls-up of it when they're brought in on a serious crime.'

'What is it you want, James?' I asked. 'I can't believe you've come all this way to try and warn me off. You must know perfectly well it won't make any difference. Oh, and by the way, are you interested in pop music, I mean, do you play the guitar or anything?'

He didn't even blink. Perhaps he had known what was coming or perhaps he really was as innocent as he looked. 'Why d'you want to know?'

'Oh, no particular reason. Someone sent me a cassette.'

'What of?'

'That's just it. It was a recording of a recording, or I suppose it could be an amateur group, although they sounded reasonably professional.'

He looked a little uneasy. 'So you'll be round at the house again. How much has Sally told you about our father?'

'Very little. I expect she finds it painful, talking about him.'

James gave a kind of snort, then turned it into a cough. 'I was wondering how much you knew about the circumstances of his death. I don't suppose it's even occurred to you that what happened to Sally could be connected to my father's so-called accident.'

He had taken the trouble to track me down, but he still felt obliged to maintain his confrontational manner.

'Look, James, if there's something you want to tell me, why not just say it straight?'

'Whose side are you on?'

'I'm not on anybody's side, I'm trying to help Sally.'

'Oh, for God's sake, you just want her to come up with something you can pass on to that half-witted Inspector. If they'd found out who killed my father none of this stuff with Sally would ever have happened. You'd never have been brought in on the case.'

My phone was ringing when I reached the flat. It was someone who wanted to send me a brochure about alarm systems. He had all the facts and figures designed to scare potential customers into handing over excessive amounts of money, but I put the phone down in the middle of his spiel. Then it started ringing again.

'Yes.' I didn't really think it was the same man, pretending we had been cut off, but neither did I have time to adjust my exasperated tone of voice.

'Dr McColl? This is Stephen Bryce. Look, I realize I've no right to phone you at home. As a matter of fact I was surprised you were in the book, I thought you'd be ex-directory, and in case you think I'm checking up on my wife, this has absolutely nothing to do with Ros.'

'Good.' To my surprise Ros had made another appointment, in a fortnight's time, but I wasn't going to tell Stephen about it.

'Anyway,' he said, 'now that Ros is your patient it would be quite wrong for me to have any contact with you, as a client I mean. That's why I decided to phone you at home, rather than at the office.' He cleared his throat. 'The reason I'm ringing...it's about Tom Luckham. I know your main concern is what happened to Sally, but now you've met the family you must have realized how shattered they are, not just by Tom's death but because the coroner at the inquest got it all so terribly wrong.'

'If you know something, you should go to the police.' But he had no intention of being put off by my tone of voice.

'There's someone I'd like you to meet,' he said, 'a girl Tom was helping at the time of his death. She lives in Eastfield, in a hostel that provides temporary accommodation for single mothers and their babies.

I call round now and again, just to see how she is. I feel I owe it to Tom. Anyway, when I saw her yesterday she told me something I think might be important.'

'What?'

There was a short pause. 'Her name's Clare Kilpatrick. Look, if I could think of any other way... I told her how you've been interviewing Sally, how you've connections with the police, and I got the impression—'

'Why can't she talk to the police herself?'

'Oh, she'd never do that.' He cleared his throat again. 'I could pick you up in my car, it wouldn't take long.'

What game was he playing? Since giving up his job he must have found it hard to adjust to having so much spare time. Was the retired clegyman, who had agreed to fill in until a replacement was found, aware that the ex-vicar was still visiting parishioners? I made a few more token protests, but I knew I was going to give in to Stephen's request, although 'giving in' was hardly the correct way to describe my increasing interest in Tom Luckham's death.

'Not this evening,' I said. 'Tomorrow, seven-thirty, but I won't be able to stay long.' I had nothing else planned, it was just a feeble way of keeping the upper hand.

'Thanks.' He sounded inordinately grateful. 'Well, I'll see you tomorrow then and, don't worry, I haven't the slightest intention of asking you about Ros.'

After he rang off I found the old Morocco-bound Bible my father had given me when I was still at school, and looked up St Matthew, chapter five, verse forty-four. Ros Bryce had quoted the right chapter, but the wrong verse. Verse forty-four had a rather different message from the one about letting your light shine before all men, but it was unlikely that her mistake had any particular significance. I read it aloud, remembering the long-ago days when my brother and I had sat between our parents on a shiny wooden pew, standing for the hymns, kneeling for the prayers.

Love your enemies, bless them that curse you, do good to them that hate you, and pray for them which despitefully use you, and persecute you.

If Ros Bryce was trying to tell me something, was it about Stephen or Tom Luckham? Or was she thinking about herself?

Chapter Eight

Plenty of clients were late for their appointments but only Lloyd was always exactly seven minutes overdue each time. With another client this might have been something we discussed, but Lloyd, who was sixteen, would have insisted, to his last dying breath, that it was just that he was bad at timing things and had forgotten to look at his watch.

I could hear him on the stairs—he never bothered to tell Heather he had arrived—and a moment later he knocked loudly on the half-open door, strode into the room and slumped in a chair.

'Take a look.' He started unbuttoning his shirt. 'Best it's been for weeks.'

It was true. The area under each armpit that he had picked raw had receded until each of the sore places was less than the size of a small saucer.

'You win,' I said. 'Still, I doubt if it'll last. You've had a good week but you'll find it difficult to keep it up.'

He looked at me suspiciously. 'Some kind of trick, ain't it?' Then he grinned. 'Had your hair cut. Makes you look dead sexy. Hey, I was going to ask you—most women, what do they like, a bloke who tells 'em what's what, or one what does what he's told?'

'Is that a serious question?'

'Well, they can't have it both ways.'

Things were following the normal pattern. Lloyd took the lead, trying to provoke me, then claiming that since I was a psychologist he ought to be allowed to say whatever he liked.

'To get back to your chest, Lloyd, how was it you managed to leave the scabs alone for two whole weeks?'

'Did what you said. Fixed me mind on something else. That film where the guy rapes this woman and she catches him and locks him in a cage. Seen it?'

'Yes, I saw it.'

'What she done to him, I mean, humiliating him like that and—'

'What d'you think he'd done to *her?*' I had fallen into the trap again. 'Anyway, I'm glad your skin's healing up so well.'

'Yeah but it don't solve nothing, do it? Don't explain why I started picking at it

137

in the first place.'

'No, that's true, but it could have started with a rash or a minor injury and the habit caught hold.'

For some reason, mention of the rape victim had started me thinking about the woman who had stolen my bag. Every so often the incident came back into my mind; it had left a nasty shocked feeling that was taking a time to fade. Was it even remotely possible that the thief and Sally Luckham's 'abductor' were one and the same person, and if so, could that person also have been responsible for sending the cassette?

One of Lloyd's boots was resting on the table. He followed my eyes, then laughed, withdrawing his leg and sitting with his knees pressed together. 'Thought since I was here, seeing you, that meant what I done to meself must be psychological.'

'What I said, if you remember, was that it could mean you were under some kind of stress.'

'Oh, I'm that all right.' He jumped up and pressed his face to the window. 'What you said—you could find the cause, what started it off in the first place, or you could find a way of getting rid of the habit.'

'Exactly.'

'So let's find what done it. I reckon it's my brother. He keeps me awake half the night, snoring and other stuff. Reckon if you told my mum I needed a room of my own.' Suddenly his voice had gone quiet and the hand inside his jacket had started scratching at his shirt. 'Reckon if you wanted you could talk to her about some other things as well.'

We were on our way to Eastfield. The sky had clouded over and the temperature had dropped a little, but it was still unpleasantly humid and Stephen Bryce's car, an old Nissan Sunny, didn't appear to have much in the way of ventilation.

'The house belongs to a charitable trust,' he said. 'It was set up to provide short-term emergency accommodation for single mothers.'

'Yes, you said. So how come Clare Kilpatrick has lived there for nearly a year?'

'I imagine the trust found they couldn't stick to the "short-term" rule too rigidly. Not much use housing people, then making them homeless all over again. They own houses in various parts of Bristol

—Birmingham, Knowle, Bedminster. My church used to make an annual donation.'

'And that's how Clare met Tom Luckham?'

'Oh, good heavens, no, she used to come to the youth club. Tom organized outings for some of the kids. Trips to the theatre, pop concerts, sporting events.'

'I hadn't realized she was so young.'

Stephen glanced at me and the car crossed the white line, narrowly missing a van coming in the opposite direction. 'Sorry. Yes, she's only seventeen. Got pregnant when she was still at school. Shame really, she was doing quite well.'

'But she decided to keep the baby.'

'Yes. Yes, I suppose that's right. I was going to say she must have left it too late, but a girl like Clare, she's not exactly your helpless, hopeless type. Listen, I wanted to ask you something, then I'll never mention it again.'

'About your wife?'

'It's just—if you think she's in a bad way—I mean, you would tell me—if you thought she was going to do something stupid.'

'You're still her next of kin. I think it's highly unlikely, but I suppose I would if

I was that worried. And the same would apply if I thought Ros needed to know something about you.'

He turned round, surprised. 'I'm not depressed. Should I be? The book was a nine-day wonder and it's not even selling that well, but I said what I wanted to. I've no regrets, it's just a question of deciding what I'm going to do next.'

He kept glancing at me, then back at the road, and I had a feeling he was preparing himself to say something else. About Ros, or was it something about Clare Kilpatrick? He was wearing a black sweatshirt that made him look unhealthily pale. I wondered if he was eating properly or if he lived off a diet of sandwiches, with the occasional take-away. There were several questions I would have liked to ask, mostly about the rumours surrounding his resignation, but he would think I had been nosing around, looking for dirt. Instead I asked where he had worked before he came to Bristol.

'Before I came to Bristol?' he repeated. 'School chaplain, up in Shropshire.'

'I should think that might have suited you.'

'Why d'you say that?' He slowed down,

turning into Henleaze Road. 'Boys aren't interested in theological discussions, except at the simplest level. Ros enjoyed it, at least I think she did. She's more adaptable than I am—most women are, wouldn't you say? Looking back, I realize I got ordained to please my mother. Stupid. Of course, it wasn't something I was aware of at the time.'

He had this way of belittling himself while making it sound almost like boasting. It was not his words so much as the tone of voice he used. *See what a hopelessly confused character I am, but don't you find me fascinating...*

'At the time of your resignation I expect your congregation had mixed feelings about what had happened,' I said, then because it sounded as if I had been doing some investigating behind his back: 'I'm just going on what my father told me. He attended your old church last weekend.'

'Mixed feelings? Oh, I suppose there were some who thought I should have stuck it out, argued my case more vociferously.'

'But you wanted to leave.' It was a statement, not a question. I was only going on what he had told me the first time we met, but he took it badly.

142

'Look, I don't know what you've heard, but if you think I've been hiding something from you... Oh, I know when people get divorced they often describe the breakdown of the marriage as "amicable", but in my case, my divorce from the Church, well, it really was. You're the expert, but I suspect when I wrote the book I was really looking for a way out.'

We had pulled up outside an Edwardian semi. There was off-road parking for two cars, but one of the spaces had been taken by a green van.

'Each resident has their own small flat,' said Stephen. 'Well, it's more of a room in actual fact, but with a basin, electric kettle, you know the kind of thing. Then there's a communal room so the mothers can meet up. And a play room, I believe. They're very lucky.'

'That's one way of looking at it.'

He had taken his jacket off the back seat and was searching for something in one of the pockets. I wanted to ask what his flat in Kingsdown was like. After living in a vicarage it must seem odd being confined to a couple of rooms, but compared with the loss of status, and of any real purpose in his life, the change in living accommodation was probably the least of his worries.

He found what he was looking for and held it up: a velvet caterpillar, joined together in four brightly coloured sections. 'As you know, I have no children,' he said, 'but it doesn't take too much imagination to realize the problems involved in bringing up a child on your own, especially when the father doesn't want to know. The baby's a boy, called Cain. For some obscure reason people seem to like biblical names these days.'

'Yes, so I've noticed.' I was thinking about Sally Luckham's guinea pigs. Matthew, Esther and Salome, the one her father had given her shortly before he died.

Stephen had jumped out of the car and pulled open the passenger door. He eyed me a little anxiously, wondering if opening the door for a woman was likely to earn him a harsh rebuke, then gave a small, relieved grin. 'Look.' His face was very close to mine. 'I'm sure you had a better way to spend the evening but this shouldn't take long.'

'I thought they tracked down fathers these days,' I said, 'and deducted money at source.'

144

'If they know who the father is.'

'Does Clare know?'

He ignored this, pushing open the wrought-iron gate, then returning to the car to make sure he had locked both doors. 'I think it'll be best if I get her to tell you what she told me, in her own words,' he said. 'I'm a reasonably good judge of character and I think she's telling the truth. Besides, what reason would she have to concoct such a story out of the blue? But I'd like to know what you think.'

'Yes, all right but I still don't understand why she waited six months to tell you.'

We were standing in the front garden, a square of concrete with a small flower bed in the centre, containing a single standard rose that had finished flowering. At the side of the house, halfway down a narrow path, a white-haired man was up a stepladder, trimming a buddleia. Stephen raised a hand to him, then turned back to me.

'Clare'd had some kind of trouble over her benefit and, in her mind, the benefit people and the police seem to amount to much the same thing. You know, anyone in authority.'

145

'So what's happened to make her change her mind?'

'I'm not sure. Look, I'm not trying to tell you how to do your job, but I think we should tread rather carefully, let Clare take the lead.'

'I'm not here to do my job,' I said. 'I just want to make sure none of this has any connection with Sally Luckham's attempted abduction.'

'Or the missing girl. It's just possible something might come out that would help the police trace Geena Robson.'

I looked up, surprised he had remembered the name.

'It's been in and out of the local paper,' he said, sounding a little too off-hand. 'Do the police have any new leads? I just keep praying the poor child's still alive.'

Was I imagining it, or were his eyes open rather too wide and, when they met mine, was his stare a little too unblinking?

A thin, dark-haired girl stood by the open front door. She had a baby resting on one hip and she was eating an iced lolly.

'We've come to see Clare,' said Stephen. 'She's expecting us.'

The woman looked at us blankly, then hoisted up the baby and strolled away

146

towards the back of the house. I heard a door slam, then a voice raised in anger. A child started to cry. I thought I heard a slap.

Stephen bounded up the stairs ahead of me and when I reached the top he was standing outside one of the rooms with his hand poised, ready to knock.

'It's me, Clare.' His voice had an irritatingly wheedling tone, the kind some social workers adopt when visiting a less than welcoming client.

The door opened but no one came out to meet us. I could see a cot in the far corner of the room, with a mobile of rabbits suspended above it, but the baby was lying on his back, on the bed, with one arm flung up above his head and the other half across his face. A voice called: 'Well, come in if you're coming,' and when we stepped inside, a girl wearing a very short skirt with bare legs and feet was draping a wet cot sheet over the back of a chair.

Stephen started to make introductions, but Clare cut him short. 'One of you can sit on the end.' She pointed towards the bed. 'And the other over there.'

Stephen shot towards the bed and poised himself uncomfortably on the pillow. I sat on a chair near the window. Clare positioned herself cross-legged on the floor.

'This is Anna,' said Stephen. 'You remember, I told you how she's a psychologist and she's been talking to Sally Luckham.'

'Best stay up here,' said Clare. 'If we go downstairs the others'll be listening in.'

'Yes, good idea.' Stephen seemed keyed up, excited, and, from the expression on his face, I had a feeling it was not just because Clare had important information to reveal. She was very attractive. Her ash-blonde hair looked natural, and her eyes were an unusual greeny-grey colour and had thick fair lashes. Her short white top revealed most of her midriff, and she was in the process of arranging her few inches of skirt. Before we arrived she had been painting her toenails. One foot had been completed but the other had three more nails to go and the bottle of pale pink varnish was beside her on the floor.

'All right, Stephen?' She spread out her legs, crossed her ankles and leaned her back against the wall. 'So what is it I'm supposed to do? Tell this lady what I saw? Except there's not that much to tell. Knew Tom, did you? Poor bugger, all those things he did to help people, then he goes and kills himself.' She noticed my face and laughed, realizing she had made it sound as if Tom Luckham had committed suicide. 'No, I mean the accident.'

I nodded and she looked at Stephen. 'What you told her?'

'Nothing. I was leaving it up to you.'

'Yeah, well, what d'you want to know?' She was enjoying herself, enjoying being the centre of attention. 'All I said was the day it happened, the day he died, I saw someone in the passenger seat of Tom's car.'

'What time was it, Clare?' Stephen knew the answer but wanted me to listen to Clare's exact words.

'About ten to eight, bit earlier maybe. I was taking the baby to the nursery, only I'd left early 'cos he'd been yelling his head off since six and I couldn't stand the noise.'

'And you saw Tom drive past,' Stephen prompted.

'Hang on, I haven't got to that yet. It was starting to rain so I was trying to get my umbrella out of the bag, only one of the spoke things had broken and got all caught up, otherwise I'd never have stopped. It was down the end of the road, not the road I was walking in, the other that goes across. I wouldn't have noticed except he had that great big car.'

'Old Rover,' Stephen explained. 'Go on, Clare.'

'Thing was, he was going that way.' She waved her arm in a direction that might have indicated south-west. 'So he was on the other side and the passenger was closest to me.'

'Yes of course,' said Stephen encouragingly. 'How much did you see of him, if it was a him?'

She stood up to check the baby. 'They mustn't get too hot—little kids. Not too hot, not too cold, not too fat, not too thin. It was still quite dark, so as I said, I couldn't see that clearly. Might've been one of those blow-up dolls for all I know, except why would Tom want one of them? Never any shortage of females happy to have a lift in his car.'

Stephen gave a tolerant smile. 'I thought you mentioned something about a hat or a scarf.'

'Could've been. Didn't see the hair properly, but you don't see much when a car goes zooming past like that. Unless there's something out of the ordinary. Dark hair I think it was, only I s'pose it could have been covered up, by the scarf. From a distance Tom's hair looked like...I mean, it could have been fair hair, not grey, well, some of it still was.'

'Stephen said you'd only remembered all this quite recently,' I said.

She frowned. 'Never said that. Just didn't seem all that important. Like I said, people often had a lift in Tom's car.'

The baby was making sucking noises. She picked him up and handed him to Stephen, then sat on the floor again and started screwing the top back on the bottle of pink nail varnish. 'If you must know, I thought the person in the car might be someone I knew, and don't ask me who 'cos I could be wrong and it wouldn't be fair getting everyone talking and all the time it had been a mistake.'

Stephen glanced at me. The way he was holding Cain it looked as if he was used to handling him, playing with him. How often did he call round to see Clare? Was it just possible... Then it occurred to me that all vicars had experience of babies. They held them over the font and baptized them, splashing them with water, cooing over them at garden fêtes.

'If you know who was in the car,' said Stephen slowly, dangling the velvet caterpillar in front of the baby's face, 'I think you owe it to Tom to tell us.'

Clare shrugged. 'Doesn't mean whoever it was had anything to do with the accident.'

'No, of course not, but at the very least that person needs to be eliminated from enquiries.'

'What enquiries?' Clare stood up in one movement, without putting her hands on the floor. 'I'll think about it, right? Only I'm not making any promises.' She took the baby and held him above her head. 'There's a girl come to the day nursery last week, got twins only one of them's got something wrong with its foot. They can put it right, it's nothing serious.' She gave me a defiant look. 'Put him in a day nursery, I do, so I can go out to work.'

'Yes. Good idea.'

'You think so? Better than being stuck with me all day. Hey, you never answered when I asked if you'd known Tom well.'

'No, I never met him,' I said.

'But you've met Erica. God, what an old bag. Still, I s'pose in the circumstances...

152

Easy to judge people, then find you never really knew what the fuck was going on.' She laughed, holding the baby so close to her body that he let out a kind of gurgling squawk. 'Got to give him a bath, unless one of you two wants to do it. No? Well, they don't know what they're missing, do they, Dumbo?'

'Don't call him that,' said Stephen.

'Why not? Oh, you think I meant... Don't be so daft. Brilliant, he is, months ahead of what he's meant to be. Dumbo, the Flying Elephant, got ears like Prince Charles. They can pin them back, you know, but what's the point? In good company, ain't you, Dumbo?' She picked up a towel that was lying on the floor. 'Kids, they're what matters, ain't that right, Stephen? Without them there'd be none of us left in a hundred years' time.'

When we left, the man who had been tying back the buddleia was cutting the front hedge. He approached us, wiping his forehead with his sleeve and leaving an earthy smear.

'Been visiting Clare,' said Stephen.

'Don't think we've met.' The man had turned towards me. His face was deeply lined and his hair was pure white, but on closer inspection he was probably only about sixty. Stephen made the introductions and it transpired that the man was a regular attendant at his old church. Wesley Young. The name rang a bell.

'Wesley looks after the garden here,' said Stephen. 'Can't think how you find the time.'

'Nothing to it. Don't know a thing about flowers but I'm all right with shrubs. Just keep cutting them back.' When he laughed his eyes almost closed. 'And it gives me a chance to keep an eye on Clare,' he said. 'I do it to please Marion. She has the boy now and again, but not as much as she'd like.'

'You're not the Mr Young my father met?' I asked. 'He was staying with me last weekend and, after the morning service, he had a cup of tea in the church hall. He mentioned he'd been talking to a Mr and Mrs Young.'

'Is that right?' Wesley thought about it for a moment. 'Interested in cooking? Told us he'd joined a special class. And photography too if I remember rightly, been looking for a medium-format projector for him for his slides.'

'Yes, he's been wanting one for quite a time.'

'Don't produce that many,' said Wesley. 'Most people want a thirty-five mill.' He had started picking up the lengths of buddleia that had landed on the path and laying them in a heap on the concrete. 'Call round at the shop some time and I'll see what I can do.'

'Antique shop,' explained Stephen.

Wesley rubbed his hands on the sides of his trousers. 'Antiques is putting it a bit grand. Cheltenham Road, just past the station. There's a bloke I know might have just what you need. Would've asked him before only didn't seem much point when I didn't have your father's address. I tell you what, leave it a day or two so I can ask round a bit.'

Back in the car Stephen started explaining how Wesley and Marion's teenage daughter had died the previous summer.

'Yes, my father said something about it,' I said. 'What happened?'

'Terrible thing. Killed herself, after the A-level results came out. They put too much pressure on children these days. I don't know if you agree, but I think all those league tables have added to the

155

general atmosphere of competitiveness.'

'There's always been pressure on kids,' I said. 'Do they have any other children?'

He shook his head and we sat in silence for a few moments, thinking about the loss of an only child. Then I asked how long Stephen had known Clare Kilpatrick.

'I told you how she used to attend our youth club. Even after she'd given up coming regularly she used to drop in now and again. She was one of the ones who helped Tom paint a mural on the wall of the coffee bar. He drew the figures and some of the kids painted them in, more or less to Tom's specifications. He was a very clever artist, could turn his hand to just about anything.'

'Did James help?'

Stephen turned his head sharply and his voice was unnaturally high-pitched. 'James? I believe he's inherited his father's talent, or perhaps Tom taught him how to draw when he was still a small child, but no, James would never have taken part in anything like...' He broke off, pretending all his concentration needed to be focused on the flashing amber light on the zebra crossing. When the traffic moved on his tone of voice had returned to normal. 'I keep forgetting you've met James. What did you make of him? I imagine he's the type girls fall for by the dozen.'

'I've no idea,' I said. 'If they do I should think he gives them hell.'

Stephen laughed, relieved that my opinion of James appeared to be no better than his own. 'To be honest, I hardly know him. Tom was always very loyal, but reading between the lines I think there were tensions. He was worried James seemed so aimless, so uncommitted to any kind of a career. You know, some of Tom's paintings were extraordinary, very original, but also accessible to ordinary people who know next to nothing about modern art. Of course it's pretty well impossible to make a living out of painting, not that his prints were anything to be ashamed of—there's four of them in the foyer of that new hotel—but I imagine from Tom's point of view they were rather formulaic. Italian-style courtyards, with long shadows and plants in pots, you know the kind of thing.'

I was only half-listening. The rest of my brain was remembering the scene on Coronation Road, just past the garage, where the road bends twice, then straightens out as it approaches the underpass. James Luckham wheeling a buggy and a small blonde-haired girl hanging onto his arm. I was almost certain the girl had been Clare Kilpatrick.

Chapter Nine

Five to nine on a rainy Wednesday morning, and as soon as I walked into the building Heather rushed out of her office to ask if I could phone Mrs Bryce. 'It sounded urgent, Anna.'

'But she didn't say what it was about?'

'Not really. Something to do with her friend?'

I groaned. This had happened too much recently. One client, leading to another, leading to yet another. Sometimes it was as if it only took one person to discover the Psychology Service, and the cries for help from their friends and relatives became an epidemic.

'I'd better find out, then,' I said, wondering why Heather looked so preoccupied. 'Is everything all right?'

Her fingers left the keyboard and started drumming on the surface of her desk. 'Yes. I mean, no. It's just—well, Dawn upset me a bit but I'm sure she didn't mean it.'

'What did she do?'

159

'She didn't *do* anything. It's the way she talks to me as if I'm an inferior being. No, don't say anything to her, that would only make things worse.' She reached out to pat me on the arm. 'Why not use this phone to call Mrs Bryce? It'll save you going all the way upstairs.'

It rang for a long time. I was just about to replace the receiver when Ros Bryce came on the line, breathing hard.

'Oh, thank goodness. It's Livvy. The friend where I'm staying. Livvy Pope. She's done something rather stupid, I suppose I ought to call the doctor, but she's begged me not to and—'

'What happened?' I sat on Heather's desk.

'Cut her wrists,' said Ros. 'Well, one of her wrists. Oh, not deep cuts, just a series of little nicks, but it made me realize how unimportant my problems are. Livvy's the person you ought to be seeing.'

'You'll have to phone her doctor.'

'No, I told you, she won't let me, and really there wouldn't be much point. I put antiseptic cream on her arms and she's in bed now, resting, but I wondered if you could possibly come round later on.'

My first reaction was to say that

that would be quite impossible, then something—perhaps it was simple curiosity —made me hesitate. Ros had known Tom Luckham. Did she also know Clare Kilpatrick? And perhaps there were things she could tell me about the rest of the Luckham family. When she came for her appointment I would have to let her talk about whatever was on her mind, but if I called round to see what I could do for her friend, the visit would be on my terms, I would be doing her a favour.

I was due to see Sally Luckham the following day, ostensibly to find out if any more forgotten memories had come to the surface, although this time I had a personal, as well as a professional, interest in seeing her. Tom Luckham's death was starting to prey on my mind. I had met people like Clare Kilpatrick before, people who were adept at getting the maximum number of people at their beck and call. She could easily have made up the mysterious passenger in Luckham's car. On the other hand, Stephen Bryce seemed to think she was telling the truth.

'She must have medical attention,' I told Ros. 'Provided she's had a visit from her GP I'm prepared to see her once, mainly for your sake, but I can't promise there'll be any follow up treatment.'

'Yes, I understand.'

'I'll be with you at about six o'clock then,' I said. 'Oh, hang on, I'd better write down your address.'

Miller's Cottage was the last house in a long terrace, with a stream running between the pavement and the front gardens. The rain had cleared. I left the car in a lay-by and started walking back towards one of the small wooden bridges. Willow herb grew everywhere, in large purple clumps, but the surrounding grass had been trimmed quite recently and still had marks where the lawnmower had cut too deeply into the soft turf. The stream ran the whole length of the road and most of the cottages had names like Brookview or Watersmeet. The village was almost exactly midway between Bristol and Bath. Houses, even very small ones, were expensive, and since these were picturesque and, if you liked that kind of thing, highly desirable, Livvy must have money. Had Ros Bryce mentioned anything else about her? Perhaps she had a well-paid job, although the few remarks Ros had made about her had given the impression she was at home most of the time.

A woman was coming out of her front door, carrying a small baby under one arm, and holding a toddler by the hand. I thought about Clare Kilpatrick, and remembered how Stephen had handled her baby so naturally and seemed genuinely fond of it. Was it really possible he was Cain's father? I had dismissed the idea almost as soon as I had thought of it—someone like Stephen would be unlikely to leave the mother of his child living in a hostel, even if it was well run with good facilities—but the arrangement could be just temporary, until he had found himself a proper place to live. Was it because of the baby that he had resigned from his parish? His wish for me to meet Clare might have had nothing to do with Tom Luckham. Did he need someone to talk to and was he preparing me for his confession? And what about Ros? Tom Luckham could have threatened to tell her about Clare and the baby, and Stephen could have...

Endless speculations were a waste of time; I needed more hard facts, but for the next hour or so I would have to try and concentrate on Livvy Pope and why she had decided to mutilate her wrist. Attempted suicides, where the patient never had the least intention of doing him or herself any real damage, tended to exasperate everyone involved. Another person, who might be considerably more unhappy, had to wait his or her turn before receiving anything in the way of professional help, whereas there was something about physical injury, however slight, that meant action had to be taken immediately.

Through the thick bottle glass in the front door of the cottage I thought I could see a figure in a nightdress descending the stairs. Ros had seen me coming and the door was opened just as the figure reached the bottom. I heard Ros shout Livvy's name, then she put out her hands as if she thought she was going to fall.

'Do come in,' she called, then, turning back to Livvy. 'At least fetch your dressing gown. No, wait, I'll get it.'

When I entered the tiny hallway Livvy was still standing at the bottom of the stairs. Keeping her eyes averted, she squeezed past me, flattening herself against the door, then hurried on towards the kitchen, where I could hear her turn on a tap. The musky scent of her body spray or deodorant lingered in the air.

'I'm so sorry.' Ros had a pink dressing gown over her arm. 'Where's she gone? Oh, she's in there. D'you mind? I expect you'd like to see Livvy on her own, only...'

'Let's just see how it goes. The doctor's been round?'

Ros nodded. 'Didn't get a very good reception. Dr Gallagher, do you know him? Nice man. I told him you were coming.'

Livvy was winding a gauze bandage round her left arm. Her long white nightdress and shoulder-length hair made her look like the subject of a Pre-Raphaelite painting and I had a feeling the effect could well have been intentional. She looked up briefly, her lips slightly parted and her eyes open very wide. Everything about her exuded self-pity, but she was more like a character playing a part than someone who was truly unhappy. No, that was unfair. I was making a snap judgement on the flimsiest of evidence. Even so I had a struggle to stop myself labelling her *hysteric personality* even before we had been introduced.

'Anna McColl,' I said. 'Would you like some help with that?'

'Thank you.' As I had expected, her voice was a whisper. She stood perfectly still, like a small child, and I started winding the absurdly long bandage round her left arm. 'The doctor said there was no need for bandages but they feel so sore. You must think me very weak, but I felt so...so...'

'Angry,' said Ros.

'No, not angry,' said Livvy. 'Powerless.' Her eyes met mine, but only for a fleeting moment. 'I write,' she explained. 'Mostly poetry, but some prose too.'

I fixed the end of the bandage with the small gold safety pin Ros had taken from her pocket, and stepped back to inspect my handiwork. 'Why don't you sit down and tell me about it?'

'Shall I?' Ros hovered by the door, but Livvy shook her head.

'No, don't go away.' Livvy turned towards me but kept her eyes focused on the table. 'I've talked to Ros for hours and hours, she's been wonderful, but she thought I ought to see a professional, in case I'm clinically depressed. Isn't that what they call it?'

166

'You've been feeling very depressed. Did something happen this morning, something that made you—'

'No, nothing. I mean, nothing except what was going on in my mind.'

For what seemed like quite a long time the three of us sat in silence. Once or twice Ros opened her mouth, but I signalled to her to let Livvy find her own words.

'Tom,' she said at last, 'I was thinking about Tom. Did you know him?'

'Tom Luckham,' Ros mouthed.

'No,' I said, 'I never met him.'

'But you've heard about him.' Livvy's tone of voice suggested that everyone must have heard of such an amazing person.

'You were very fond of him?' I said, and as she slowly turned her head towards me I realized she was a good deal older than I had first thought. In her late forties or even her early fifties. It was the childlike appearance that had made me think she was younger. Not just the nightdress and fluffy bunny slippers, but the white hair band and long straight hair.

'Tom was my mentor,' she said. 'He believed in me. In my work. He said it was a waste just showing the poems to friends, they needed a wider audience. When the

167

first book was accepted he explained how the publishers would need a little money, mainly because poetry never has very large sales, and of course I wanted the best quality paper and binding. You see, they told me the poems were of an exceptionally high standard and warranted a really good edition.'

Ros and I avoided each other's eyes. Was it possible Livvy really believed what she was saying?

'Would you like to see it?' She rose slowly to her feet and opened a drawer in a Welsh dresser, pausing for a moment, like an actress making her first entrance in a play, then taking out a book and placing it in front of me so that its edge was exactly in line with the side of the table.

'It's beautifully bound,' I said insincerely, although it was true, the binding at least was of fairly good quality. The first poem was called 'Wintertime'. I scanned the words, taking in the usual rhymes: trees and breeze; frost and lost. 'I'm sure they're very good. Have you been writing recently? Sometimes it can help the grieving process.'

I dislike expressions like 'grieving process' but there was something about Livvy

Pope that made it difficult to empathize. In such a situation I often find myself resorting to jargon.

'Oh, I write all the time,' she said. 'Don't I Ros?'

Ros nodded, keeping her lips pressed together, and glancing at the electric kettle. It had boiled, and switched itself off, and her natural instinct was to make tea or coffee, but she was wondering if it would be inappropriate. Then she noticed my expression, gave a faint smile of relief and started collecting up cups and saucers.

'Tell me about Tom?' I said, unable to take my eyes off the hard ridge of Livvy's collar bone protruding over the top of her nightdress.

'Tom.' She spoke the word softly, hanging on to the last consonant as though she was practising her diction. 'How can I describe him? He was an artist, extraordinarily talented, although those stupid people in London never properly appreciated his work. Can you imagine having a gift like that and still finding time to do so much for others?'

Ros cleared her throat. From the look on her face she had listened to all this more times than she cared to remember.

I wanted to spare her another eulogy but if I said anything she might think she was in the way.

'Your arm,' I said. 'Have you done anything like that before?'

Livvy flinched, as if I had broken a spell. 'Before? No, never. They say physical pain can bring relief from mental suffering. It's so difficult to explain. I was...I felt as if I was in a trance, as if someone else was telling me what to do, as if it was meant.'

'And when you realized what you'd done?'

'I was horrified, so ashamed. If Ros had been out I dread to think what might have happened. She was quite cross with me, but I expect that's a natural reaction, isn't it?'

An exceptionally large spider was crossing the floor towards us. Neither Livvy nor Ros seemed to have noticed, but Livvy struck me as the kind of person who might have any number of phobias. I stretched out my foot and the spider took a right hand turn and disappeared under the Welsh dresser.

The kitchen was like something out of a Habitat catalogue. Bunches of herbs hung from hooks in the wall and the mantelpiece was covered with glass jars, full of dried beans and lentils. The white walls contrasted with the red tiled floor, and every piece of furniture, apart from a solid fuel stove, was made of old pine. There was no sign of a fridge or washing machine; presumably they had been consigned to a utility room so as not to spoil the effect.

'Perhaps if you tell me a little about yourself,' I said.

'Me?' said Livvy, as if she was the last person I had come to hear about. 'Well, I'm... No, I don't suppose my age is at all relevant. Ageism, I loathe it, don't you? All "isms" are destructive. All generalizations. I mean, we're all individuals, aren't we, so—'

'Have you got a job?' I said, breaking my usual rule that the client must never be interrupted. What kind of a rule was it, anyway? Interruptions often served a useful purpose.

'A job,' Livvy repeated. 'I thought Ros had explained I write.'

'Yes, of course.'

She smiled faintly. 'Poetry, prose, a radio play. They never actually broadcast it, but

171

there was a lot of interest. Of course, I'd wasted nearly two years, living with a community in the North of England. The leader of the movement was such a charismatic person, but it's wrong to follow a leader, isn't it? You have to work out your own destiny, through meditation and by immersing yourself in the real world.'

Ros was making tea. She had her back turned and her head thrown back a little. 'Livvy has a son,' she said. 'He's called John and he's working in Spain.'

'Yes, that's right.' Livvy sounded grateful to Ros for reminding her. 'Gavin, my husband, died when John was eight. We might have been destitute, he was never good with money, but fortunately my parents had left me just enough to live off, provided I'm careful with my accounts.'

'Tell Anna about the nightmare you had,' said Ros. 'I found Livvy on the bathroom floor, must have been last Thursday, no, Friday. She'd walked there in her sleep. She'd been dreaming about a cave—going into a cave then finding the entrance had been blocked by a fall of rock.'

Livvy leaned towards me, cupping her

chin in her hands. 'It was so awful,' she said, 'the worst nightmare I've ever had. Stephen was with me. You've met Stephen, haven't you?'

'Ros's husband?'

'Me and Stephen, alone in the dark in this horrible place with doors that opened onto steep drops, hundreds of feet below, and shadowy figures lurking at every...' She broke off, looking at Ros, then back at me. 'Of course, I know why Stephen was there. He's often in my dreams. You see, it's easy for Stephen to understand how I feel. We have so much in common. We both loved Tom.'

Ros walked back with me to the car. Nothing was said about Livvy's dream or the fact that she and Stephen had both 'loved Tom'. If Ros wanted to talk about it that was up to her, but I doubted if the remark had any great significance, apart from the fact that it indicated a degree of aggression on Livvy's part.

'Livvy's very angry,' I said, 'isn't that what you think?'

'Most of the time she just seems depressed but every so often she has a little outburst, breaks something, throws a cup across the room. To be honest with you, I find it almost a relief.'

'Yes, I can imagine. Does she say why she feels so angry?'

'Not in so many words. About the accident, I imagine, about losing Tom.'

I had my car keys in the lock but I didn't want the conversation to end. 'Some people seem to think there was something odd about the accident.'

Ros put out a hand to steady herself against the car. 'What people? Is that what Stephen told you? Or Sally? She was so attached to her father. Is she all right? Are they all all right?'

The woman I had seen leaving her house was coming up the street, pushing a double buggy, the kind where one child sits in front of the other, rather than side by side. As they drew level the baby in the back section reached out to take hold of the toddler's ear, and the quiet street was rocked with savage screams.

'Did Stephen mention a girl called Clare?' said Ros, and it was almost as if she had waited for some diversion, some extraneous noise, before she found the courage to put the question.

I nodded, trying to work out what to

say next, playing for time, waiting for the buggy to pass. 'Yes, he mentioned how Tom Luckham had helped her when she had to find somewhere to live. Incidentally, d'you know if she and James are friends?'

Ros looked blank. 'James? Oh, you mean Tom's son. Well, if they are, I can't imagine how they met. James took care never to go near the church. We met him, of course, when we were round at the house, but if Tom was enthusiastic about something you could be sure James would avoid it like the plague. Sad really, I believe he's quite a talented artist.'

There were so many questions I wanted to ask. What was her opinion about the accident on the Mendips? How had she felt about Tom Luckham? Was she aware that Erica was drinking heavily, and if she was, did she feel it her duty to do something to help, or had she and Erica never been on particularly good terms? What did she think about Livvy's book of poetry?

Livvy was standing in the doorway of Miller's Cottage, waving frantically. Ros reacted as a mother might if she saw her child about to cross a main road without looking.

'Don't let her turn you into her slave,' I said.

'No. I ought to find somewhere else to live, I know I should, but just at present it all seems like too much effort. I don't know if you've noticed, but people seem either to play the role of the helper or the helped, and of course it's no use the helpers complaining because the reason they help so much is because they can't bear to feel indebted.'

'Are you talking about yourself?'

She laughed and her rather plain face suddenly looked quite attractive. When she recovered from the break-up of her marriage and decided what work she was going to do, I hoped she would allow herself a new hairstyle and something a little less dowdy in the way of a wardrobe.

'I'm not talking about being a vicar's wife,' she said fiercely, 'or the fact that I denied, even to myself, just how much I disliked it. No, what I mean, the dependency thing, it's like that in marriage, wouldn't you say, never an equal partnership. So-called equal partnerships simply lead to endless arguments about who's caring for who.'

Livvy, still in her nightie, but minus

the dressing gown, was running across the grass. When she caught up with us she was out of breath.

'Look, I wanted you to see, I thought it might help.' She held out a photograph in a silver frame—the head and shoulders of a man with a handsome but reddish face, greying hair, and thick tufty eyebrows.

'You can tell so much from a face, can't you?' she said, almost losing her balance in her excitement. 'You can't hide yourself, your face tells the world what you are. I know it sounds sacrilegious but sometimes I thought Tom could have been the new Messiah.'

Chapter Ten

'We'll have to sell the house,' said Erica. 'It's not just the upkeep, the council tax is exorbitant. Besides, I need the cash.'

'I'm sorry.'

'Oh, it's not the house.' She sipped her colourless drink. 'Just the thought of estate agents, solicitors, all that frightful business.'

Kicking off her shoes, she crossed to the patio doors and peered into the garden. 'I'm so sorry to keep you waiting. Sally nipped out to the local shop to buy some bits and pieces.'

'That's all right,' I said, wanting to make the most of our time alone together. 'So she's feeling better, doesn't mind going out on her own? Only last time I was here she said she felt too nervous to visit her friend.'

'Mmm?' Erica seemed to have no interest in what I was saying. 'Tom paid all the bills,' she said, running her tongue round the rim of the glass. 'I expect you'll think me very old-fashioned, but I preferred it that way. Naturally, I had accounts at several of the large stores, but as far as everyday things were concerned—well, he was so much more organized.'

'You must miss him.'

'You see, I've never had a job. You probably find that odd too. We were living in France when James was born. It suited me rather well, even better than it suited Tom, as a matter of fact. In those days...' She stood up and fetched a bottle of tonic water, adding a dash to her drink. 'Of course, it's not easy being an artist these days. I mean, it's all been done before, hasn't it. Representational, abstract, conceptual, and now with computer graphics you can just twiddle a few knobs or whatever it is they do and, hey presto, instant art, just like Andy Warhol wanted us all to do!'

'Is that one of your husband's paintings?' I asked, pointing at a large expressionist landscape, with solid blocks of colour, more or less representing the sky, the sea, and a headland. I was sure there had been no painting on that particular wall the last time I visited the house, but perhaps I had been too preoccupied to notice.

'He was quite well thought of at one time,' said Erica, draining her glass. 'Oh, I'm so sorry, would you like to join me?'

'No, thank you.'

'No? I often wonder how we're supposed to live. Animals—I mean, other animals— well, it's survival of the fittest, isn't it, but can we really be so different? All this making allowances for people, understanding them, it's an American idea I always think. They'd raised their standard of living as high as it could go, then realized people still got unhappy so decided they'd better start all those God-awful encounter groups and clinics where some psycho-fool thinks he can see inside other people's heads.'

I had no feeling that she was getting at me, it was just the ramblings of someone whose blood was kept permanently topped up with alcohol. But perhaps I was wrong. Perhaps she knew exactly what she was saying and the slurred talk was just a way of opting out of any responsibility for her choice of words.

'We lived near Axbridge,' she said. 'Did I tell you that before? Tom was still only in his late thirties and if anything growing a little older had made him even more attractive. Silly to marry such an attractive man. Better to have a mad, passionate affair, then settle down with someone with a pleasant, reliable face.'

'The day your husband died,' I said, watching her carefully, ready to change the subject if I felt I was causing her unnecessary pain. 'I believe he received a phone call quite early in the morning.'

'Is that what Sally told you? There's a phone in the hall.' She jerked her head towards the door. 'And another upstairs. Tom answered the downstairs one.'

'You were still in bed?'

She screwed up her face in a deliberate scowl. 'And I didn't listen on the extension if that's what you were thinking, so there was nothing any of us could tell the police.'

'Your husband seems to have had a lot of friends.'

'Oh, he did,' she said vaguely, 'lame ducks and arty types, rather an odd mixture don't you think? I think he wanted me to join the C of E but somehow I never quite got round to it. Not that you have to actually do anything. Just go to church, I suppose. Perhaps not even that. Sally was nine when it happened

181

so James must have been just fifteen. Doing all those prints—I suppose, looking back, it was the beginning of the end. I thought his painting meant everything. I used to model for him, did I tell you, yes, I'm sure I did. Of course in those days.' She patted her stomach. 'They say people only remember the happy times, but I've never found that to be the case. Oh, I suppose when we lived in France...'

'I met Clare Kilpatrick,' I said. Perhaps, in the circumstances, it was not the most tactful thing to say, but she was becoming maudlin and that never did anyone much good. 'She said your husband had helped her a lot, found her a place to live.'

'Kilpatrick. Doesn't ring a bell. One of Stephen's parishioners, is she?'

'She's got a young baby. A boy called Cain.'

'Cain? Sounds like a garden chair. Oh, Cain, as in the Bible, killed his brother, didn't he, or was it the other way round?'

James was standing in the doorway. He had a piece of toast and marmalade in his hand and the marmalade was sliding over his fingers. 'Sally heard Dad's end of the call. You know that, Mother, only she couldn't remember a bloody word, not a single bloody word.'

So he had been listening outside the door for several minutes.

'Don't talk like that, darling.' Erica stretched out an arm and James moved towards her, cramming the remains of the toast into his mouth, then wiping his hand on his T-shirt.

'I thought you'd come to talk to Sally,' he said, glaring at me. 'My mother hasn't been well.'

Erica's eyelids drooped. 'Dr McColl's only doing her job, James. If she's going to help Sally she needs to know as much as possible.'

'About Dad's accident?' He stressed the word *accident*. 'But one thing leads to another and by the time she's finished the whole bloody family will have been psychoanalysed. Anyway, she's not here to help us, she's working for the pigs.'

Erica laughed, leaning back in her chair and lifting both feet off the ground. 'You'll have to excuse my son, Dr McColl. He believes in doing your own thing, and that usually includes being extremely rude.'

James was standing by the window. He felt in the pocket of his jeans and took out a handful of coins. 'Col needs paying,' he said, 'how much have you got in your bag?'

'Oh, not today, love. I gave my last fiver to Sally.'

'If he's not paid soon he'll leave.'

'No, he won't, he loves coming here.'

Erica had an amused expression on her face, but James reacted angrily. 'Oh, don't talk such rubbish. Why d'you have to make everything into some kind of stupid...'

'Hush, darling, not in front of our visitor.'

James had left the window and was sitting on the arm of his mother's chair. I thought about the cassette with its dreary numbers about women who led men on, then let them down. Had it been James who sent it, and if so did it have some special significance I had failed to appreciate?

'You want to know about my father?' he said suddenly. 'How would you describe him, Mother? Larger than life? He liked to be on the go all the time. Artists are usually introverts.' He raised his head to look at me, and for once his expression was fairly pleasant. 'Dad liked plenty of people around. He was a diabetic but he never let that interfere with anything he wanted to do.'

'Yes, I suppose that's a fair description.' Erica reached for a decanter and poured out what was left, splashing a fair amount of it on the carpet.

'If you have a lot of friends you're going to have one or two enemies,' said James, standing up, listening. 'Sounds like Sally. Look, why don't you go and lie down for a bit, Mother. I'll stay here and make sure she's OK.'

Erica held out her arms to be pulled to her feet.

'Will this be your last visit?' she asked, lurching towards me, then regaining her balance as James leapt forward to help.

'I'm not sure. I shall have to talk to the police, but if Sally's remembered everything she's likely to, I hope I won't have to trouble you much longer.'

'Oh, it's no trouble,' said Erica. 'Apparently Ros Bryce can't speak highly enough. You've certainly made a conquest there.'

Fay Somers had invited me to dinner. As I drove out to Eastbury I tried to make sense of my latest conversation with Sally. She had seemed nervous, on edge, made a huge effort to convince James she was all right and there was no need for him to stay in the room, then kept glancing towards the closed door, as if she thought someone might be eavesdropping. At one point she had scuttled across the room and yanked it open, but there was no one there.

She had told me the colour of the car, now she was not so sure. And the smell of perfume—she could have imagined it. If she had to go to court would they make her swear on the Bible? Supposing she had remembered wrong?

'You only have to speak the truth,' I said. 'If you're not sure you can say so.'

But nothing I said seemed to reassure her. When I told her it was time to stop she looked relieved, then made me promise I would come back in a few days' time.'

'I mean, I might wake up in the night and find something had come back to me.'

'Yes, I suppose that's always possible.' I decided it would be unkind to point out that if she did remember anything important she could always phone the CID. She looked so pale and anxious. When I first came to the house she had seemed afraid of me. Now she seemed to see me as an ally, someone who would protect her from the police, give her some moral support.

As I was leaving, a car drew up and Ros Bryce climbed out, looking grim-faced, then, when she saw who I was, seemed distinctly uncomfortable. Quickly adjusting her expression she walked over to tell me how much better Livvy was feeling.

'It was so kind of you to come all that distance, Anna. I do hope you don't feel I put any pressure on you. I was thinking, I have an appointment with you next week but do you think Livvy could have it instead?'

My instinct was to refuse. I had no wish to see Livvy again, whereas Ros was someone I felt I could help. On the other hand, from Ros's point of view, finding someone who could see Livvy was probably the thing that would help Ros herself the most.

'Yes, all right, if that's what you want.'

She hesitated, afraid she had annoyed me. 'I'll bring her, if you don't mind. Otherwise I doubt if she'll come.'

'Whatever you think best.' I started winding up the car window. 'I'm sorry you've had to deal with all this, just when you needed some peace and quiet.'

Turning the corner, I slowed down, and was just in time to see Erica coming out of the house. Were they old friends? I doubted it. They were too different, one who had chosen to anaesthetize herself with alcohol, the other grimly determined to fight on, even though her life too had been turned upside down...

I drove past the turning to Fay Somers's road and had to reverse into a side road, then return the way I had come. I had been invited to dinner and it was only after I had accepted the invitation that I had learned that Fay's landlady had also been invited, as her husband was away on business. Fay thought it would be fun—*we three girls*—but I was afraid the whole evening might turn out to be a bit of a bore.

I was late. Before leaving home I had been attempting to fill up the space on an airmail letter to Owen. Martin's shingles and the fact that Dawn Rivers seemed to be going from bad to worse had covered half a side, but what else could I tell him? Explaining my involvement with the Luckham family was too complicated, quite apart from the fact that Owen resented what he referred to as my 'suspiciously stormy' relationship with Superintendent Fry.

I thought about Howard and how I would have to tell him Sally had changed her mind about the colour of the car. It would have the effect of making him doubt everything she had come up with so far. I would be reminded how there was still no lead on the missing girl, how any day now another girl might be abducted, and how the Assistant Chief Constable had been pinning his hopes on, as he called it, 'a cure for Sally's amnesia'. But it wasn't amnesia. As far as I could tell, she had recalled everything she had taken in at that time. Some children have eidetic imagery—they can see an image of a picture for forty-five seconds after it is taken away from them and report it in detail—but Sally showed no signs of having this ability. Her conflicting accounts of the event could be put down to a generalized fear, or a dread of having to appear in court. Or was it possible—something she always denied vehemently—that she believed her assailant might discover she had provided a good description and lie in wait for her?

The house where Fay was staying was halfway up a hill. There was nowhere to park so I drove on until I managed to find a side road not exclusively allocated to house-owners with permits, then started walking back.

I had forgotten the name of Fay's landlady. Jane? Judy? It turned out to be Jill, a woman in her forties who looked faintly familiar, although it was clear she had never met me before. Perhaps she reminded me of someone else. Fay introduced us, telling each of us a few facts about the other. *Anna's a clinical psychologist. She lives in Cliftonwood and I met her friend, Owen Hughes, when I was back home.* Then it was Jill's turn to be described. *Jill runs a day nursery for kids from birth to four years old. There's a waiting list as long as your arm but they're restricted by limitations of space and the staff they can afford to pay.*

'We get a small grant,' said Jill, 'and various charities help, but really it's something the council should have taken over long ago.'

'Oh, you wouldn't want that.' Fay was passing round glasses of icy cold white wine. She was dressed in a rather unflattering skirt that had been gathered in a bunch at the waist, and a brightly coloured shirt with a pattern of fishes and

190

waves. In contrast, Jill's clothes were in various shades of grey: light grey cotton trousers, held up by a dark grey belt, and a plain grey T-shirt with a V-neck. She was very thin, with tiny breasts and incredibly thin arms. It occurred to me that she could even be anorexic, but if that was the case would she have agreed to eat a meal prepared by Fay?

'Listen,' Fay was saying. 'I'm not great shakes as a cook but I can manage a seafood pasta. On the other hand, if anyone's allergic to squid I can always rustle up some alternative dishes.'

Jill and I both made the kind of appreciative noises designed to reassure the cook, then Jill started asking about my work.

'There's three of us,' I said, 'but Martin, who's in charge of the unit, is off sick at present.'

'That must be difficult.'

'Yes, they've let us have a replacement, someone called Dawn, but of course it's hard for the clients who were seeing Martin.'

'Dawn,' Jill repeated. 'I knew a psychologist called Dawn Rivers.'

'Yes, that's the one.' I felt a twinge of guilt.

Jill blushed, putting up her hand to cover the cheek nearest to me. Had she been one of Dawn's clients?

'Your husband works for a bank, doesn't he?' I said, changing the subject.

'Financial services. He's on a course, learning how to make even more money for the bank, persuading people to invest in unit trusts.'

The rest of the house had been very quiet, then a sudden burst of music shattered the silence and Jill sprang up and made for the door.

'Oh, leave them,' said Fay. 'When they've made their point they'll turn it down, you'll see.'

Jill glanced at me, then sat down again. 'I'll slip down later,' she said, 'just to make sure they're in bed. I expect Fay told you I have two boys, Alistair and Neil. I'd have loved a girl, but there you are, can't have everything.'

'Oh, but they're sweet boys,' said Fay.

The noise had been reduced to a steady beat and a droning voice.

'This nursery you run,' I asked, 'I suppose people have to leave quite young

192

babies with you so they can go back to work?'

'Sometimes it can't be avoided. I try to encourage mothers to stay at home for the first three months, but that's not always possible, especially since most of our clients are single parents.'

'But not all?' asked Fay. 'I thought they'd get first choice and that would just about fill up your list.'

Jill started to explain how they also took children from families with particular problems, like a mother or father with a serious disability, or a parent in prison, and at that point I interrupted to say I had met Clare Kilpatrick quite recently and she was full of praise for the day nursery.

'You know Clare?' Had I imagined it, or was there a touch of anxiety in Jill's voice?

'I've only met her once,' I said. 'She told me about a man called Tom Luckham and how he had befriended her, helped her to find some accommodation.'

'Tom died.' Jill was speaking to me, but looking at Fay. 'He used to raise money for the housing trust that owns the house where Clare lives. She was very upset about what happened. I think he meant a lot to her.'

What was she trying to tell me? I had imagined the mothers dropped their children off at the day nursery at eight to eight-thirty, then collected them again around five o'clock. It surprised me that she seemed to know so much about Clare.

'You must get to know some of the mothers quite well,' I said.

'Sorry?' Jill pretended not to have heard, although she had been listening intently. 'Yes, I suppose that's right. If there's a new problem it's vital we hear about it—for the sake of the child.'

Fay was looking a little uneasy and I wondered if Jill had mentioned Clare and Tom Luckham before and, if so, had she said something less than complimentary about Tom? Perhaps Jill had objected to my mentioning Clare, although talking about a particular mother whose child attended the nursery could hardly be seen as breaking a confidence, particularly since I had told her Clare had raised the subject herself.

'That reminds me,' said Fay suddenly, only what it was that had reminded her seemed a little obscure. 'The missing

194

schoolgirl, is there any news? Do the police have any idea what could have happened?'

'I'm afraid not,' I said. 'They're just hoping she's still alive.'

Some of Jill's wine splashed onto the table. 'Alive? Oh, I don't think there's much chance of that. My son's at the same school, although not in the same year, of course, and from what he's told me she was a quiet, sensible girl, not at all the type who'd have disappeared without telling anyone where she was going.' She glared at me, then looked away. 'Do you have any children?'

Coming from someone who had only just met me, it was a reasonable question, but I was pretty certain she knew the answer already. What was she saying? That I might be well versed in all the theories but she was he one with hands-on experience of children and how they were likely to behave?

Fay came to the rescue. 'Anna's done some fascinating research into why people confess to crimes they haven't done,' she said, filling up Jill's glass, then leaning across to check mine.

'Really!' Jill sounded falsely interested.

'That among other things,' I said. 'Now,

tell me how you organize your nursery. How on earth do you manage, caring for tiny babies and energetic toddlers, all in the same place?'

The rest of the evening went reasonably well. Fay's food was good, if a little too bland for my taste, and she had certainly gone to a great deal of trouble. Now and again I tried raising the subject of Tom Luckham's accident, but Jill always managed to move quickly on to another topic. Any mention of Clare Kilpatrick was met with the same response, although I had the feeling Jill knew something about her that could be important. Sensing a degree of tension between us, Fay kept raising more and more points of intellectual interest—how much of our intelligence is innate, how much a result of our early environment. Is most psychological research into the children of single parents distorted by the fact that such children are more likely to be economically disadvantaged? Jill always came up with politically correct opinions, which had the effect of making me take the opposing viewpoint, and, but for Fay, who insisted on calling each imminent row 'a fascinating exchange of ideas', the evening could have been a disaster. Both Fay and Jill came to the front door to see me off, then Fay offered to walk to where my car was parked.

'This Tom Luckham,' she said, 'He was the diabetic you mentioned that time in the pub? Tell me it's none of my business but is there some mystery surrounding his death?'

'The police don't think so.'

'But you do.'

I shrugged. 'He seems to have been a person who had a strong effect on people. There are those who think the accident could have been investigated more thoroughly, but since the post-mortem provided no evidence of foul play it's hard to know what the police were supposed to do.'

'And you, Anna, what do you think?'

'I'm trying to keep an open mind,' I said. 'Too many rumours floating around, too many people who may have axes to grind.'

We had reached my car and I thought someone had scraped paint off the passenger door, but it turned out to be a trick of the light, a reflection from a flickering neon lamp.

'I tell you what,' said Fay conspiratorially, 'if I get the chance I'll ask around a little.'

'Yes. Fine.' I wondered who she was going to ask, but since she seemed to pride herself on her tact and diplomacy, she was unlikely to do any harm.

'Jill's a sweetie,' she said, 'but her marriage is going through a bit of a rough patch and to compensate she gets herself a little too involved with her mothers.'

'You mean the mothers of the children at the nursery?'

Fay nodded. 'Don't say anything. As if you would.' She gave me a quick kiss on the cheek. 'Thank you so much for coming round and, as I say, if I hear anything I'll be in touch.'

It was nearly half past eleven and the man from the video rental place was on the phone. It took me a moment to take in what he was talking about.

'You're telling me I took out a video and failed to return it?'

'Had it three days, love. Tried to reach you before but you were unavailable.'

Surely he could have left a message on the answering machine. 'But I haven't been to the shop for well over a month.'

'On the computer, love. Have to pay for it, I'm afraid.'

'Why should I pay when I haven't..' Then it dawned on me. The day my bag was taken my membership card had been stolen, along with all the other stuff. 'Look, were you there when the video was taken out?'

'Could've been. Couldn't really say.'

'Only my membership card was stolen. Yes, I know I should've told you but it never occurred to me... Listen, you can't remember what the person—'

'Sorry, love, I could ask Lorraine but she's not here at the moment. Afraid you'll have to pay the nine quid just the same.'

'I know, but the thing is—'

'Oh, don't worry, love, we'll cancel the card, give you another.'

'Yes. Thanks.' No point in explaining the money was the least of my worries. 'I'll be back to talk to Lorraine. Will she be there tomorrow?'

'Make it after six.'

'Yes, all right. Anything she can remember, absolutely anything. It's really important I find out who took out the video.'

Chapter Eleven

'We're expecting the worst,' said Howard. 'Sally Luckham's description was our only lead. Now she's changed it so many times it's virtually worthless.'

'But you don't even know if the two cases are linked.' I had come to talk to him about Tom Luckham, but I was wasting my time. 'This girl I mentioned,' I said, 'the one who says she saw someone in the passenger seat of Mr Luckham's car.'

'It was six months ago, Anna. If the girl thinks it's so important why didn't she come forward in January?'

'I suppose she's only just realized Tom Luckham's death might not have been an accident.'

Howard sighed. 'And who put that idea into her head? Look, if you'd concentrated on Luckham's daughter...I don't want to cast doubts on your special techniques but I'm starting to wonder if a subtle psychological approach has any better effect that Ritsema's heavy-handed tactics.'

'Thanks.'

'Yes, well...people breathing down my neck, a mass of conflicting reports. Ken Robson, the girl's father, received an anonymous letter saying Geena was living in Glasgow.'

'So that means there's a chance she's still alive, or was it like the silent phone calls Graham Whittle was telling me about?'

'Since it was addressed to "The Pervert" it seems likely it was just another sick member of the public trying to insinuate Robson had something to do with his daughter's disappearance.'

'But you don't think he's involved.'

Howard shook his head. 'We've interviewed both parents several times. Unless they're exceptionally good liars.'

'Which they could be.'

He sighed. 'Your expertise includes spotting when someone's making a good job of covering up the truth? We're not too bad ourselves. For a time Ritsema had an idea one of Geena's teachers knew more than she was letting on, but there's not a scrap of hard evidence.'

I stood up, ready to leave. 'So you're not interested in Tom Luckham?'

'Can't afford to be, Anna. The man's

been dead six months and unless you can bring me something more than a vague memory resurrected by a seventeen-year-old girl...'

'I'm seeing Sally Luckham once more,' I said. 'No, don't tell me it's a waste of time. There's something going on in that family, something I don't understand.'

Howard opened a drawer, pulled out a pad and started writing. 'This girl who thinks she saw someone in Luckham's car, you say her name was Kilpatrick?'

'Clare Kilpatrick.'

'And she lives in Eastfield. Perhaps I should have her address.'

I hesitated. 'What are you going to do?'

'Nothing, for the time being, but I'll read through the file if it'll put your mind at rest.'

'Thanks.'

'You're welcome.' He smiled, and to my annoyance I found myself looking away, then fidgeting with a paper clip on the desk.

'No news about your handbag, I'm afraid.'

'No, well there wouldn't be, would there? Someone nicked my membership card, took out a video and failed to return it. Now I'll have to pay nine quid.'

He opened his mouth, but I got in first. 'Yes, I know I should have reported it missing, but would you have thought of it?'

'Probably not.'

I moved towards the door and Howard followed me, reaching out to turn the handle. I could feel his breath on my neck. He smelt of soap.

'You cancelled all your credit cards,' he said.

'Yes, of course.'

'Good.'

'Right, well if I get any more out of Sally I'll be in touch.'

'Good.' He still had his head turned away. 'Heard from Owen recently?'

'Yesterday.' I had the letter in my pocket, three sheets of airmail paper that provided little in the way of information and even less in the way of an expression of affection. 'Seems to be enjoying himself, although the work he intended to carry out appears to have met with some kind of hitch.'

'When's he due back?'

'In a month or so, depends on how

much data he manages to collect.' I started down the corridor, expecting Howard to accompany me, but when I turned remembering how I had intended to ask him if he knew whether Erica Luckham had already been a heavy drinker at the time of her husband's death, he had gone back into his room.

Ros and Livvy were sitting side by side in the waiting room, both reading magazines. As soon as Ros saw me she stood up and gave me a questioning look.

'I could easily stay down here, but Livvy says she wants me to—'

'No problem,' I said, holding the door to let them pass. 'If that's what Livvy would prefer.'

Livvy smiled faintly. She was looking better but still had the same wistful, martyred expression that had irritated me so much the first time we met. Once inside my room I rearranged the chairs so that the three of us were sitting roughly in a circle. I asked Livvy to describe how she was feeling.

'Oh, you know.' She lifted a hand to touch her hair and the long flowing sleeve of her Indian smock was displayed in all its shimmering glory. 'I suppose I'd thought this room would be larger, and there's no couch for people to lie on, or am I terribly out of date, is everything quite different these days?'

I dug my nails into the palms of my hand. What was the point in agreeing to see the woman if I was incapable of controlling my dislike of her? Why had I agreed to the appointment? Because I was so bad at saying 'no', so easily seduced into thinking I was indispensable?

'Let's go back to last Tuesday,' I said. 'You were alone in the house?'

Livvy was staring through the window, but Ros nodded. By her expression she had made it clear that she preferred not to join in verbally, but the occasional nod was permissible.

'I suppose I must have been,' said Livvy. 'I'm so sorry, but do you think I could have a glass of water?'

When I returned with the water I could hear whispering that stopped abruptly as I entered the room.

'Thank you so much.' There was a welcome edge to Livvy's voice. Something Ros had said to her? Whatever it was that had brought about the change, it provided

205

a faint hope that the real Livvy might be going to put in an appearance.

Sitting up straight she crossed one leg over the other, and started inspecting the sole of her sandal. 'It was because of...I suppose I'd been thinking about...'

Ros was breathing hard. Her fingers drummed on the arm of her chair. She caught my eye and pushed her hands into the pockets of her fawn cardigan.

'Sorry,' said Livvy, 'only it's so important to choose the right words.'

'Yes, I understand.'

'Oh do you, I'm so glad. The doctor wanted me to see a psychiatrist, but when I told him I had appointment with you... Grief, it's a strange thing. No day is the same as the one before. I read a book about the four stages, I think there are four. Denial and disbelief, then anger. Why me? Then...I suppose the next part is the one everyone understands. Misery, a terrible feeling of loss. What's the last stage?'

'Acceptance,' I said, then realizing I sounded a little hard, 'which is not necessarily to say the feeling of sadness is any less.'

There were tears running down her

face and, for the first time I felt some genuine sympathy. This was real pain. She found a tissue in the purse that was hanging round her neck on a plaited rope. 'Tom helped me so much. He was a saint. No, I really mean it. He worked for the Samaritans, then it came to him that he wanted to do more, to devote the rest of his life to helping people.'

'How did you meet him? You'd known him for quite a long time, had you?'

'Sorry? Oh, Tom, how long had I known him? I used to live in a flat overlooking the Downs. I attended Stephen's church. I mean, I'd started attending it long before Stephen became the vicar.'

'And that's where you met Tom?'

'He could have been a great artist, but he gave it all up to live a genuinely Christian life.' She picked up the glass of water which, until that moment, had remained untouched. 'If we all helped each other, took more trouble, stopped leading such selfish lives and...'

Ros could contain her frustration no longer. 'Tom was a failed artist, you know that, Livvy. After the bottom fell out of the prints market he had to find another way to make himself feel important in the world.'

Livvy swung round, still holding a tissue to her nose. 'No! How can you say that? I don't understand.'

'Yes, you do, you just don't want to face the truth. It's easier to idealize people —some people are wonderful, some people are no good at all—but if we're honest with ourselves it's very rarely that simple.'

The passive expression on Livvy's face had disappeared, along with the breathy voice. 'Just because you were jealous of him and Stephen,' she said, speaking almost without opening her mouth. Then she suddenly relented. 'No, I didn't mean...I'm sorry, Ros, it's just, hearing you talking about Tom like that. I suppose when someone has such a strong personality... Am I right, Dr McColl? If a person is so well loved there are bound to be people who resent it. Oh, I'm putting it awfully badly. What I meant to say...'

Her eyes were fixed on the opposite wall and she seemed to be waiting for me to make some comment. Was it true that Ros had resented Stephen's relationship with Tom? I remembered Stephen's remark about how Ros felt Tom had influenced his decision to leave the Church. Had Tom encouraged Stephen in his feeling that he was unsuited to being a parish priest? Although Ros preferred to concentrate on Livvy's problems it was clear that her own life had been turned upside down. She had no home of her own, no job, no children: the parish had been her life. Where had she been at the time of Tom's accident? According to Stephen's account of that day, she would have been alone in the vicarage while he was up in London, using his day off to visit some specialist bookshops.

'Right,' I said, 'you're both feeling upset, but perhaps that's not such a bad thing. I suppose what I need to ask you now, Livvy, is do you want Ros to stay for the rest of the session or would you prefer—'

'Yes, of course she can stay.'

Ros was half out of her chair. She sat down again, but only on the edge. 'I think it might be better if I waited downstairs.

'No. Please.' Livvy wailed. 'I'm sorry, it was just what you said about Tom, only I know you didn't really mean it.'

'No, of course not.' For reasons of her own, probably because she disliked the fact that I had witnessed her anger, Ros had decided to return to her usual survival tactic: humouring Livvy, treating her like a small child. Had Livvy been in love with Tom? Love, infatuation, obsession, what was the difference? But if she believed Tom had felt the same way...

The rest of the session consisted in my attempting to draw Livvy out, and persuading her to talk more freely, with Livvy countering all my efforts with meaningless remarks about the cleverness of psychologists and how she might even study psychology herself, with the help of the Open University. After that she insisted on running through a list of the people whose lives Tom Luckham had managed to turn around. A man with multiple sclerosis who was desperately lonely until Tom found him a female companion who had lost her husband and needed someone to fill the gap. A married couple who were going to split up until Tom persuaded the wife that her husband and children were more important than her career. When the last 'case' was mentioned, Ros glanced at me and pressed her lips together and I wondered if she was thinking that some of Tom's attempts to 'do good' had meant imposing his own values on people with very different ideas about how they should run their lives.

After the two of them left I collapsed in my chair, exhausted. It had been a mistake, allowing Ros to stay in the room. She had come to give Livvy moral support but she was not a disinterested observer and, in some way I couldn't yet understand, Livvy's relationship with Tom Luckham seemed intimately tied up with what had happened to Ros and Stephen. I tried to make my usual notes, but Ros's remark kept going round and round in my head. *Tom was a failed artist, you know that, Livvy. After the bottom fell out of the prints market he had to find another way to make himself feel important in the world.* Had something happened that no one wanted to talk about, something connected with Tom's death, some incident that had taken place shortly before the accident?

The video shop was packed. I queued up behind a man who wanted three videos but one of them had turned out to be unavailable, in spite of the fact that its case had been displayed on the rack. After several minutes of pointless argument, my frustration overcame me and I interrupted his outburst with one of my own.

'Look, I need to speak to the woman who works here most evenings. It's important and I haven't much time.'

The man behind the counter tried to ignore me, then decided that it was going to lead to more trouble than it was worth, and turned to call through a door at the back. 'Lorraine! Someone to see you.'

A head appeared. 'Who is it? What do they want?' She approached the counter and I raised my hand to get her attention. 'Listen, I'm sorry to bother you, but someone stole my membership card and took out a video they never returned.'

For a moment her face looked blank, then she clapped her hands together. 'Oh, it was you, love. I'm sorry, but if you're expecting me to tell you who it was I'm afraid I haven't a clue.'

'You can't remember anything?'

'No, I didn't say that. In the ordinary way I doubt if I'd have noticed. It was the video that made me give her the once over. Middle-aged, she was. Well, I daresay she wasn't that much older than I am, but the kind who's not interested in how she looks if you know what I mean.'

I nodded encouragingly. This certainly

wasn't the case with Lorraine. Her salmon pink eye shadow contrasted dramatically with her jet black hair, and she was wearing a white blouse with ruffles right up to her chin, and a red skirt that was so tight I doubted she would be able to sit down in it.

'Anything else?' I asked.

She put her head on one side and smoothed down the front of the skirt. 'Hang on, ever since Les told me what happened I've been trying to think. Had glasses, I think. Oh, and a head scarf. Funny thing to wear when the weather's so warm. Don't think it was raining that day. Sorry, love, if she'd had something particular about her... Don't remember her speaking a word, just held out the video and the card, then opened her purse and waited for me to tell her how much. Tell you what, though, she had a funny taste in videos. Took it off a high shelf.' She pointed across the shop. 'Not the kind I'd want to be seen dead with, but it takes all sorts.'

'What was it?'

'Hang on, it's on the computer, that's why Les gave you a ring.' She operated the keyboard, then waited impatiently for the information to come up on the screen. 'There you are. *The Grim Raper*. I ask you, whoever'd think up a title like that?'

Back home there were two messages on the answering machine, the first one from Chris, asking if I could go to the cinema with her the following evening, to see an old Gerard Depardieu film. The second message was from Jill Hinchliffe. *Anna, this is Jill, you remember we met the other evening. I got your number from Fay, only I wonder if you could give me a ring. Yes, well, that's it really. Thanks.* Then a number that was repeated twice, in case I missed it the first time.

When I rang back a child answered, cutting short my explanation by dropping the phone on a hard surface and shouting. 'Mum!'

I heard footsteps, then someone coughing. 'Hallo?'

'Is that Jill? This is Anna. Anna McColl. You left a message.'

'Anna! Oh, thank you so much for ringing back. Oh, heavens, I've been worrying ever since I saw you, but now I'm wondering is it better to say something or keep quiet?' She let out a long, dramatic

214

sigh. 'It's about Clare Kilpatrick.'

'Yes?'

'You know her, don't you, only I'm not sure if it's in a professional capacity or...'

'I met her through Stephen Bryce.'

'Oh, Stephen.'

So she knew who I was talking about. 'Yes, I remember you saying,' she added, although I was quite certain I had said nothing of the kind. In fact no mention had been made of how I came to have met Clare.

'Since he gave up his parish he's kept in touch with Clare,' I said, 'and some of his other parishioners I expect.'

'Yes, of course.' Was there a touch of relief in her voice? 'Only the thing is, did he mention Cain's father?'

This was getting tricky. How much did Jill know? How much did Clare want her to know?

'No, I've no idea who the baby's father is,' I said. 'I don't think Stephen knows either.'

There was a pause at the other end of the line, quite a long pause, then a child's voice called: 'Hurry up, Mum, it's your turn, we're waiting.'

'I won't say any more just now.' Jill's

voice was reduced to an almost inaudible whisper. 'It's only rumours and it wouldn't be fair, would it, only if you ever felt...'

'I'm not quite sure I understand.'

'No, I'm sorry. Having a baby when you're still at school, it's a very traumatic thing to happen, but Clare seems to have dealt with the whole thing exceptionally well. Her parents didn't want to know. There's four more in the family so I suppose they felt they just couldn't cope, but Clare managed to get in touch with all the right people and by the time Cain was born she was quite nicely set up.'

What was she telling me? That Clare was a scheming little manipulator?

'Tom Luckham,' she said, 'was a wonderful person. If anyone tells you anything different that's because really good people always make the rest of us feel a little uneasy. Oh, sometimes it's so impossible to decide what's for the best, but if you ever thought it was going to help. I don't know if you agree but some things are so important they seem to transcend any rules of confidentiality.'

I started to say something reassuring, something that would persuade her to tell me more, but she had rung off.

Chapter Twelve

The morning had gone badly. A client, who had been depressed ever since her youngest child left home, blamed me because her doctor had told her he was going to stop prescribing anti-depressants. *You must have phoned him. He used to be so kind.* Nothing I said made any difference and she had stormed out of my room, banging the door so hard that a piece of loose plaster had dislodged itself and fallen behind the filing cabinet.

The next client, a sad young man in his early twenties, insisted his panic attacks were the result of my refusal to go out with him. *Women always treat me like shit. I thought you'd be different but you've turned out just the same.*

After he left I had a go at sticking the lump of plaster back on the wall, but only succeeded in making the hole larger. I had slept badly, endlessly going over the video incident in my mind. At the time it had shaken me a little, but did it really mean very much, the fact that whoever had stolen my bag had a taste for violent, erotic movies? Taking it as a personal attack on me seemed a little paranoid—someone else quite different could have found my membership card. But a middle-aged woman with a head scarf and glasses? The woman Nick had seen in the pub? The same woman who had attempted to drag Sally Luckham into her car?

I had been trying to work out if James could be right, if what had happened to Sally was connected in some way with her father's death. What was the truth about Tom Luckham? Almost everyone I talked to had provided a picture of a successful artist who had given it all up to become an unpaid social worker. Almost everyone. Not Ros Bryce.

When I came down to the office just after midday I found Heather in tears. Eventually, when she had enough breath to speak, she explained, through the tissue pressed to her nose and mouth, that Dawn had accused her of booking in two different clients at the same time.

'It wasn't my fault, Anna. Dawn hadn't told me she'd given her ten o'clock appointment to the woman she saw last week. There was a new person already booked in at that time, but she didn't check the—'

'What did she say? Dawn—what did she say to you?' I sat on the edge of Heather's desk and picked up the stapler, moving it from hand to hand, imagining it was a hand grenade and any moment now I was going to extract the pin.

'I forget,' said Heather. 'Just a few scathing remarks and some stuff about the last place where she'd worked and how they'd had a proper system designed to avoid double-bookings.'

'Where is she?'

Heather's head shot up. 'No, don't say anything. It'll only make things worse.'

'Has Nick got someone with him?'

'No, I think he's writing a report.'

When I knocked on Nick's door it swung open immediately. He had been listening to my conversation with Heather and was ready, hands held up in mock defence.

'Leave it alone, Anna, she's only here a couple of weeks more.'

'What's that got to do with anything?'

'OK, so she's not the easiest of people,

but we have to work with her and it's no good—'

'We work with Heather, too,' I said angrily.

'All right, you do whatever you want, only don't expect me to take sides. Anyway, maybe it *was* Heather's fault, maybe she should've told her about the new client.'

He was right, it was better to forget it, sympathize with Heather and point out, as Nick did repeatedly, that Dawn would soon be gone. Instead, I turned his argument on its head. 'Since she'll be gone in a couple of weeks there's no point in pussyfooting around. I'm going to have it out with her.'

Nick shrugged. I gave him a withering look and started up the stairs, rehearsing what I was going to say, then the phone in my room started ringing.

'Yes.' My voice still had an edge to it, which could well account for the pause at the other end of the line.

'Is that Dr McColl? This is Erica Luckham, it's about that girl you mentioned.'

I had no idea what she was talking about, then it suddenly came to me that she must be talking about Clare. 'You mean Clare Kilpatrick.'

'Yes, that's the one.' For once she sounded relatively sober, in control of herself. 'When you asked I never made the connection, then later I realized you must have meant the child who helped Tom paint the mural, then became a bit of a pest.'

'A pest in what way?'

Erica cleared her throat. 'Oh, you know, got a crush on him, I suppose. Used to hang about, hoping to catch a glimpse of him, even came to the house once with some cock and bull story about a book he'd promised to lend her.'

'This was before she got pregnant?'

'I beg your pardon? Yes, of course, I'm talking about two years ago, more. Tom had to give her a good talking to, be cruel to be kind. Anyway, I thought you ought to know, just for your records.'

I had expected to find the usual clutter of chairs, tables, and old oil heaters displayed on the forecourt, but Wesley Young's place was no junk shop. The windows were crammed with telescopes, theodolites, sextants, barometers and a range of precision instruments, most of which were a mystery to me. His small green van was on the forecourt, just to one side of the shop window. It had a sign painted on the side that I had failed to notice when it was parked outside the hostel—YOUNG'S ANTIQUE AND SECONDHAND EQUIPMENT—along with the shop's address and phone number.

When I pushed open the door the place looked empty, then I saw Wesley's legs and realized he was halfway up a ladder, just like the first time I had seen him.

'You found me then,' he said, turning his head, but keeping hold of a high shelf. 'Where did you leave your car?'

'Near the park.'

'I got what you wanted.' He had a rather battered-looking box in his hand. He had seen me coming.

'A projector? That was very clever of you.'

'It was slightly damaged but tell your father I've tightened up the focusing mechanism and he shouldn't have any trouble.' He came down the ladder, took the projector out of the box and turned it upside down on the counter, studying some trade mark or patent number on the base. 'Let you have it for two-fifty.'

Presumably he meant two hundred and fifty. 'Right. Fine.' I had no idea if it was a reasonable price but it seemed unlikely that someone who knew Stephen, and knew that I knew him, would overcharge me excessively. 'Can I give you a cheque?'

'Cash would be better.' He had replaced the projector in its box and was putting the box in a carrier bag. 'Take it. You can settle up later. You're a friend of Stephen Bryce, then? Terrible for a young girl like that to be tied down with a baby.'

'You mean Clare? There's plenty more in the same situation.'

'Doesn't make it any better though, does it? Tom Luckham found her the place at the hostel. Knew Tom, did you?'

'No, I never met him.'

He leaned his elbows on the counter. He seemed in no hurry for me to leave. His chin was covered in white stubble, but the hair on his head was soft and silky, brushed forward, with no parting, giving him a rather quaint appearance, like a character in a fairy tale. 'Marion's been good to Clare since Tom died,' he said. 'Has Cain for the day if Clare wants to look round the shops at the weekend. Always been fond of kids.'

'Marion's your wife?'

'Decent chap, Tom, need more like him. Of course, some people said he should've stuck to painting, but there's always people to put the boot in. Makes them feel uneasy seeing someone trying to lead a Christian life.'

'Yes, I know what you mean.' It was odd how his words were almost a carbon copy of Jill Hinchcliffe's. Meeting all these members of the Tom Luckham fan club was starting to make me dislike the man, rather in the same way that being told repeatedly how good a particular film or television series is often produces a feeling of antipathy towards the object of so much praise.

Wesley was watching me, wondering what I was thinking. 'This business with Sally Luckham, d'you suppose it was the same person as took the other little girl?'

'The police think it's possible.'

'Must be, I suppose. Be a strange thing, wouldn't it, two perverts in the same city, at the same time.'

I nodded. 'Sometimes you get copy-cat crimes.'

'Yes, I suppose that's right. You'll have met Erica then?'

When I made no comment he laughed. 'Think I'm prying? Just enjoying a bit of conversation. Gets lonely spending all day in the shop. You know, you get an idea of a person, then something they say makes you realize you never really knew them at all.'

'Yes, I know what you mean.' I assumed he must be talking about Erica but his next comment was about Tom Luckham.

'That Pope woman thought he could walk on water. Mistake turning someone into some kind of god, wouldn't you say? Always ends in disillusionment or worse.'

'Livvy Pope?'

'Oh, you've heard of her. Thought you might have. After Tom died...maybe he'd taken on too much, worn himself out. And that business with Stephen can't have helped. Marion and I have never quite seen eye to eye about that. If anyone had asked me I'd have said he should've stayed on, stuck it out, ignored all those malicious rumours, all that—'

He broke off. A woman had come into the shop and was studying a caseful of old watches. Wesley enquired if she needed any help, but she shook her head and moved on to a display of surgical instruments and knives. I wanted to ask what he had meant by 'malicious rumours', but something in his expression made me think he had said as much as he was going to say.

'Right, well I'd better be off.' I picked up the projector. 'I'll be back with the money tomorrow.'

'No hurry, end of the week'll do.' He came round from behind the counter to hold open the shop door. 'You're a psychologist, is that right? Kind of job I'd have liked if I'd had the education. Everything anyone does, however crazy it might seem, there has to be a reason, it's just a question of finding out what that reason is.'

'Yes, I'm sure that's right.'

'So there's no such things as irrational behaviour.' He was rolling a cigarette. He licked the paper and smoothed the join, then tapped the tobacco down to one end. 'Wife doesn't approve. Still, what you don't see you don't grieve over. Two or three a day can't do you much harm, could even do you a bit of good.'

The woman who had been in the shop

squeezed past us, glancing at Wesley with the slightly embarrassed expression of someone who has failed to find what she wanted but is afraid of causing offence to the shopkeeper.

'Doreen,' said Wesley. 'Comes in most weeks, never buys a thing.' He lit his cigarette and inhaled deeply. 'Your father, he lives in Kent, is that right?'

'Near Maidstone.'

'Active in his own parish, is he?'

'He's a church warden.'

Wesley nodded. 'Good listener, like Tom. Marion took quite a liking to him.'

What was he leading up to? Then I remembered how my father had mentioned that the Youngs had told him about their daughter's death.

'He's a widower,' I said, wanting to show sympathy, but without intruding. 'My mother's death was sudden, unexpected. When something like that happens it changes people, makes them more aware of other people's suffering.'

Wesley crossed to the van, unlocked the passenger door, and took something out of the glove compartment. 'So he told you about Tricia,' he said. 'He told you about our daughter.'

'Yes, I'm very sorry.'

He nodded slowly, standing with his back against the van. 'Speaking as a psychologist would you say people ever get over something like that? No, don't bother to answer, stupid question. Tell your father there'll be no problem with the projector. Good as new.'

On my way home I drove past the hostel where Clare Kilpatrick lived. Two girls were coming through the gate, both dressed up for an evening out, huddled together under an umbrella to protect their hair from the recurrent heavy showers.

One of them could have been Clare, but when I slowed down I could see they were older, at least they looked older. I tried to imagine what it would be like, living in a hostel occupied entirely by single mothers and their babies. Having something in common, did they all help each other, both in practical ways, and with moral support, or did petty squabbles break out over who had left dirty plates on the draining board or broken the washing machine?

When I turned the corner a bus had pulled up at the stop, forcing the traffic behind it to come to a halt, and as I watched, Clare stepped off, then leaned against the shelter, searching for something in her bag. On an impulse I pulled up, a short distance away, with two wheels on the pavement, jumped out and started walking towards her. She was dressed in white jeans and a pink T-shirt and there was something different about her, but perhaps it was just that she was returning from work. I doubted if her employer would have approved of the tiny mini-skirt she had been wearing the last time we had met.

'Clare?' When I spoke her name she straightened up, turning her head in all directions, then spotted me and let out a sigh that appeared to be of relief rather than exasperation.

'Lost my purse. Must have had it on my knees in the bus.'

'Maybe someone will hand it in.'

'Some hope, couldn't lend me twenty p., could you, only I have to make a phone call.'

I opened my mouth to say surely there must be a phone at the hostel, then realized it would sound incredibly mean. 'Yes, of course.'

She took the coin, crossed the road to the phone box, then called over her shoulder. 'Don't go away, something I wanted to tell you.'

Her voice was different too. Softer, more sophisticated. Perhaps it was the effect of being out without the baby. Where was the baby?

The phone call lasted quite a time. I kept glancing at the place where I had left my car, but traffic was light and it didn't seem to be holding things up.

When Clare returned she looked happy, excited. 'That's done, then. Now, you coming in, or shall we go for a bit of a walk?'

'I saw you get off the bus,' I said.

'Oh, yes.' There was no resentment in her voice. 'Look, are you coming?'

'Hang on a minute,' I said, 'I've left my car half on the pavement. Where's Cain?'

'Oh, you remembered his name. Tracy collected him when she went to fetch her little girl. We take it in turns, see.'

'Yes. Right. So if you're not in a hurry maybe we could drive round for a bit.'

She shrugged. 'Suits me. What kind of car is it?' She peered down the road, running her fingers through the ash blonde hair that was now about half an inch long. 'Oh, not bad,' she said, 'doesn't look as if it'll conk out in the middle of nowhere.'

I drove towards Henbury Hill. By the time we had circled round the Blaise Castle Estate she would have had time to tell me whatever was on her mind and, with any luck, I would be able to ask a few questions.

'I got in touch with the police,' I said, 'about the passenger in Tom Luckham's car. I'm not sure if they're going to follow it up. I mean, I don't know if they'll actually need to interview you, but I'm sure they're very grateful.'

'Like hell they are.' She was rubbing at the condensation on the windscreen. 'All they wanted was to close the case and be done with it.' She looked at her watch. 'Cain's been playing up so I can't be long. That's the only good thing about that place where I live. Always someone around to give you a hand.'

'Yes, and I believe Marion Young looks after him now and again.'

She stopped wiping the windscreen. 'Who told you that?'

'I've just been round to Wesley's shop. He sold me a second-hand projector for my father. They're rather difficult to find.'

She wasn't listening. 'Look, I don't know much about you, only what Stephen's told me, but if you're going to find out who killed Tom you can ask me anything you like.'

'What makes you so certain he was murdered?'

'Oh, come on.' I glanced at her and she was giving me a pitying look. 'Met Erica, have you? If I was you that's where I'd start.'

'Why d'you say that?' I wanted to ask about her and James. Was she the girl I had seen in Coronation Road? I was almost certain she was, but that didn't mean she and James were lovers. Above all, I wanted to know who was Cain's father.

'Stephen's been good to me,' she said, 'but if you're thinking there's anything else... All I'm interested in is making sure the person that done it to Tom don't just get away with it. Of course, after what happened, you might be wondering why it bothers me so much.'

'After what happened?'

'Oh, just one of those things men always seem to regret, although at the time they're happy enough.' I could hear the amusement in her voice. She was enjoying keeping me guessing. 'Look, Tom's dead, that's a fact. Let's just concentrate on getting some justice for him. As I said, you want to talk to that Erica. I mean, she was married to the guy so I reckon she knows more than I do. Reckon if she wanted to she could tell you just about everything you need to know.'

'So that's what you wanted to tell me.'

She hesitated. 'Reckon that'll do to be going on with.'

The rain had stopped and as we drove past the row of trees on the edge of the estate I had to pull down the visor to block out the flickering sunlight. Clare was leaning forward, humming to herself, but when I started to ask how long she had known Erica she interrupted to say it was time to go back.

'Not thinking of abducting me, are you?'

I turned to smile at her but she had taken a map out of the glove compartment and was running her finger down the list of streets. For the next five minutes or so neither of us spoke. We both had questions we wanted to ask, but both knew we were unlikely to get satisfactory answers.

'This day nursery where you leave Cain,' I said at last, 'it's a good place, is it?'

She shrugged. 'Yeah, I s'pose, except this woman who runs it...always looking for trouble she is.'

'How d'you mean?'

'Well, take Kevin, he'd fallen over, bumped his head but nothing to make a fuss about, only the way Jill acted you'd think his mother had beaten him up. Then, there's Kim, only fifteen months she is but Jill thinks she ought to be talking, keeps asking if she's had a hearing test. I reckon she's got some book that tells you what they're s'posed to do when. Rubbish, though, ain't it? I mean, they're all different, Kim'll talk when she wants to.'

'Yes, I'm sure you're right.' Jill was only doing her job but I could imagine how some of the young mothers might find her a little authoritarian.

Just before I dropped Clare off outside the entrance to the hostel she asked me what I thought of Stephen Bryce.

'Funny bloke, wouldn't you say? Whoever heard of a vicar who doesn't believe in God?'

'I don't think it's quite that simple,'

I said. Then, aware that I might have sounded a little patronizing, 'I mean, people have different concepts of God.'

'Be keeping in touch, will you?' She had one foot on the pavement. 'About the police and everything.'

On a sudden impulse I decided to give her my phone number. 'Look, if you think of anything else and you'd rather not talk to the CID... If I'm out you can leave a message on the answering machine.'

She took the slip of paper and pushed it in the pocket of her jeans. 'See you, then. Next birthday I'm going to get Cain a car like this, only with pedals, of course. Oh, by the way, that question you were dying to ask. If I knew the answer I'd tell you, only I don't, so you're wasting your time.'

Chapter Thirteen

Stephen Bryce had left a message with Heather. She had written it down verbatim. *Tell Anna I don't want to bother her but if she has time Marion Young would like a word.* There was a number to ring and a request that I phone during the day, preferably before five o'clock.

'Mrs Pope's in the waiting room,' said Heather. 'I told her you were all booked up today but she said it would only take a moment.'

Livvy was standing behind the door. I heard her before I saw her; she was making little noises in her throat.

'I'm so sorry, just turning up like this.' She was wearing a full-length dress, made of blue and green Indian cotton, and a pair of shiny black boots with pointed toes. 'I don't want to see you. I mean I don't need... It was just... I was passing nearby and I thought you might like to see these.'

She pulled a book out of a paper bag, then pushed it back inside again. 'My later poems. I think they're better than the ones I showed you before. They were published just before Tom...' She couldn't bring herself to finish the sentence.

'Thank you.' What else could I say? 'I'll let you have it back when—'

'Oh, no, it's for you. I've several copies at home. Poetry never sells well, does it, and the bookshops these days...well, they're just not interested.'

After she left I resisted the temptation to take the poems into the office and read one or two of them to Heather. The binding was less expensive-looking than the previous volume, but the paper was just as thick. *Think Your Book Deserves to be in Print? Send no money.* Not yet. *This could be the breakthrough you've been waiting for. Thousands of satisfied customers found their lives changed dramatically with their first publication.* I'll bet.

I was expecting to find verses about *robins bobbin'* and *love from above.* Still, who was I to mock? I had never written a poem in my life—not since I was at school anyway—and the chances of finding a reputable publisher who would take on a book of *good* poetry must be extremely slim.

Livvy was out in the car park. I thought she had come on her own, but now I could see that Ros had brought her. Had they made a special journey or was the story about how she *just happened to be passing nearby* genuine? Perhaps she carried her precious books with her wherever she went.

Ros saw me through the window and waved. Livvy was already in the passenger seat, with the door closed, but Ros had a sponge in her hand and was wiping dead flies off the windscreen. If Livvy stayed in the car it might be possible to ask the question I had been wanting to put to Ros ever since she had brought Livvy for her last appointment.

'Anna, how are you?' She greeted me like an old friend, then lowered her voice and inclined her head towards Livvy. 'I'm sorry about this. It's a shame the way those vanity publishers exploit people. It was Tom Luckham who suggested she send off the poems. He said things had changed now there was so much desktop publishing, and it might be quite a decent company that charged a reasonable rate.'

'You've read them?'

Ros hesitated, looking around her as if

she thought the car park might be bugged. 'Tom used to laugh at them,' she said, her voice full of suppressed anger. 'Livvy never knew but other people did.'

'You're sure of that?'

'Oh, absolutely.' She pushed her hair behind her ears. 'You're thinking about my remark last time we saw you. No, that had nothing whatever to do with the poems. All I meant, well, if you insist on turning someone into a saint you can hardly blame them if they fail to live up to your expectations.'

Livvy was watching us. She had found a comb and was running it through her long, straight hair, slowly, rhythmically.

'So how did Tom fail to live up to Livvy's expectations?'

'Oh, you know, forgot her birthday, promised to call round at the cottage, then rang up at the last minute to say he had another engagement.' She broke off, raising a hand to Livvy, indicating that she would only be a minute. 'Anyway, read them and let me know what you think. If you want my opinion they're no laughing matter.'

I was on my way to Marion Young's

house. She had said very little on the phone, just that she would like to talk to me if that was at all possible, and it would only take a short time. I had agreed to call round at four-fifteen. Perhaps hearing about my visit to Wesley's shop had given her the courage to ask for help and meant that she felt ready at last to talk about her daughter's death. In ordinary circumstances, I would have insisted she make an appointment to see me at the office, but it seemed unlikely she would agree to do this, and I was curious to find out what she was like, quite apart from the sympathy I felt over what had happened to her daughter.

The sky was cloudless, the best day for ages. I wondered what Owen was doing and whether it was still freezing cold in Melbourne, and whether he missed me. Then I thought about Livvy Pope and wondered how someone like Ros could stand spending so much time with her. Perhaps she felt responsible in some way. Did Stephen know about the poems and how Tom Luckham had persuaded Livvy to fork out hundreds of pounds in the belief that they had been specially selected for publication? Still, provided she could afford to pay, did it really matter? Opening the book at random I had been slightly alarmed at what I found. The first poem, entitled 'Heartsease', was short, only eight lines in all, but Freud would have had a field day working out what was going on in her unconscious.

The Youngs' house was in Sea Mills and turned out to be identical to so many other houses in the city: scallop-edged lead work below the first-floor bay window, pebble-dash on the gable, and leaded glass in the front door. Two empty milk bottles had been left on a low ledge. A tabby cat, with half an ear missing, jumped over from the adjoining garden, and started rubbing itself against my leg, knocking over one of the bottles in the process, and as I bent down to stop the bottle rolling down the path the door opened and a voice spoke my name.

Marion Young looked younger than her husband but old to have had a daughter who was only eighteen.

'Do come in, it's so kind of you to call round.' She was tall and a little ungainly, with large hands and feet, and big bony wrists that stuck out from the cuffs of her flowered blouse. Her wavy grey hair came to just below her ears, and was parted on one side and held back by a metal clip. She reminded me of my father's next door neighbour, a woman called Mrs Lappin, who seemed to spend most of her time putting out food for the birds.

'If you'd like to follow me.' She pushed open a door that led through to the kitchen, then continued on into a conservatory that looked as if it had been added on quite recently, and was filled with plants, some of them on shelves, others in large earthenware pots on the floor.

'You won't feel too hot in here, Dr McColl?'

'No, it's fine. Lovely room.' The basket chairs creaked as we both sat down. The tabby cat strolled through from the kitchen, waving its tail in the air and letting out the occasional loud mew.

'You must be wondering why I asked Stephen if I could see you,' she said. 'I suppose I should have made an appointment to come to where you work, but really I only want some advice, I don't need analysing or anything.'

I smiled, but she was staring at the ground. Her hand reached out to stroke the cat, who was now lying curled up on an embroidered cushion, and I wondered if its presence might explain the slightly unpleasant smell.

'As you know, my daughter died a year ago,' she said. 'She was eighteen years and two months. She was christened Patricia Ann, but we called her Tricia. I was thirty-seven when I married Wesley. Thirty-nine when Tricia was born.'

'You must miss her terribly.'

'Yes.' But something about her matter-of-fact tone suggested she had no wish for my sympathy. 'She was a diabetic, like Tom, Tom Luckham, that's why he was such a help to her. After the A-level results came out... You see, she needed three A's but she only got two B's and a C, but it certainly wasn't for want of trying, I've never seen a girl work so hard. Maths, chemistry and biology—she wanted to be a doctor and of course you have to get the right grades.'

The cat was kneading the cushion with its claws. Marion gave it a push with her foot. 'I expect you've come across this kind of thing before,' she said, 'but recently a question's been preying on my mind. When a child does something like that is it someone's fault, something someone did wrong, or is it a sign of some inborn weakness, something that would have come out in one form or another whatever—'

I couldn't take it. I had to interrupt her flat, unemotional voice. 'No, I'm sure it was nobody's fault.' But the woman deserved a better explanation than that. 'Usually when something terrible like that happens it's the result of a combination of circumstances. Was Tricia a quiet, reserved kind of girl? People who keep their worries to themselves are sometimes at greater risk. If your daughter was very conscientious she may have put herself under too much pressure to do well. Even so, it would be quite wrong to try and apportion blame.'

'But I have to!' The loudness of her voice made the cat jump off the cushion. It passed close by, waving its tail in the air. The smell, like a row of dustbins in a heat wave, wafted up to where I was sitting.

'I'm sorry,' said Marion, nodding in the cat's direction. 'He's old, too old, should have been put to sleep long ago, but he was Tricia's and I haven't the heart.'

'No, of course not.' She had said she only wanted advice, not *analysing,* but I felt I must try to offer her some comfort. 'When someone dies in such tragic circumstances we all want to find a reason, all wish we could have done something to prevent it.'

'But there must be a reason. You see, it's Wesley I'm worried about, not me. He had no idea you were coming here and you must never tell him, it's just, I feel I must find a way of stopping him going over and over what happened, looking through photograph albums of Tricia when she was a baby, Tricia when she started at primary school. It's so bad for him. He should be getting on with his life, trying to push what happened out of his mind.'

What was I supposed to say? I could hardly tell her that Wesley's response was far more *normal*, far more likely to help him to come to terms with the tragedy, and that her way was almost guaranteed to lead to either a mental or physical breakdown.

'Sometimes it's as if he tries to make himself feel bad,' she said angrily. 'He had a little snuff box—he collects antique boxes and tins—with a lock of Tricia's hair. It must have fallen out of his pocket, oh, months back, but he will keep on about it. Only a lock of hair.' She sounded as if she was talking about a silly child.

'I expect it meant a lot to him,' I said, identifying with poor Wesley, but hoping my words didn't sound like a criticism of her.

She was thinking about something, but not what I had just said. 'Tom Luckham,' she said suddenly. 'If he was alive he'd have told Wesley to find new interests, stop dwelling on the past. After it happened Tom was devastated, but he believed like I did that God must have had a reason.'

For Tricia's death? My father had started to say something along the same lines, a week or so after my mother died, then he had noticed the expression on my face and realized it was better left unsaid.

Marion reached out to pull a dead leaf off a pale green vine. 'Not many people knew,' she said, 'but Tom had bouts of quite severe depression. He hid them, even from his family, and never let them interfere with his work, but I could tell. I was once a health visitor, you see. And Tricia knew. He used to ask her advice, mostly about Clare.'

'Clare Kilpatrick?'

'I'm not breaking a confidence when I say Clare had a very difficult childhood. Tom could tell she was going to end up in trouble, drinking too much, going around with very unsuitable people.'

So Tricia Young had known Clare. Had they gone to the same school, even been in the same class? But if Tricia had been eighteen when she died the previous July that meant Clare would have been at least a year behind.

'You've met Clare,' said Marion. 'We're very fond of her, Wesley and I, we understand her, but what she needs just now is to be allowed to run her own life.' She pulled off another leaf. 'I'm sorry, I remember telling Stephen this would only take a few minutes and here I am, jumping about from one subject to another.'

'When you say Clare needs to be allowed to run her life, do you mean too many people have been trying to help her?'

'Oh, I wouldn't say that, but she's quite a capable girl. The trouble is, she was so fond of Tom and ever since he died... And if someone puts an idea into her head she does tend to embroider it, if you know what I mean.'

It was as if she were trying to tell me something important, while at the same time making sure her remarks were so vague she could never be accused of spreading rumours.

'What kind of an idea?' I asked.

'Oh, I don't know, I just think, but of course it's only my opinion... Wesley and I are more than happy to give her all the support she needs, but it's important she starts to feel confident enough to take responsibility for herself.'

Now, what was she saying? That too much help was making Clare dependent? That I should persuade Stephen to stay away from her for a while? But if she thought he was doing too much why couldn't she tell him herself? Then it occurred to me that she might be jealous of Stephen, that she wanted anyone in a professional or semi-professional role to stay out of Clare's life and leave her and Wesley to play substitute parents.

'These stories about Tom,' she said, 'whoever started them, all they've succeeded in doing is making a lot of people very unhappy. I hate gossip, don't you? Tom didn't have an enemy in the world. If he was suffering from depression and saw it as the only way out, don't you think he deserves to be left in peace?'

So she and Wesley both thought Tom Luckham had taken his own life.

'If you could talk to the police,' she said, screwing up her face, willing me to accept the importance of what she was saying. 'Stephen says you know an inspector or a superintendent or someone. If you explain then I'm sure they'll realize Clare had absolutely nothing to do with what happened.'

'I'm sorry,' I said, 'but I'm not quite sure what you mean. As far as I know the police have no interest in Clare, apart from the fact that she thinks she may have seen a passenger in Tom Luckham's car—the day he died.'

'Oh, that.' Marion put a hand up to smother a yawn. 'Well, if that's all it is I'm very relieved to hear it. Clare's a lovely girl, she just didn't have a very good start in life.'

Any moment now and she was going to show me out of the house. Why was she being so protective of Clare? Because she had become a substitute for Tricia? It seemed rather unlikely.

'Does Clare have a boyfriend?' I asked.

'Boyfriend? Oh, no, I don't think there's anything like that.'

I wanted to tell her how I was certain I had seen Clare and James together in Coronation Road, but if they *were* having an affair and wanted to keep quiet about it, it was hardly up to me to give away their secret.

A dreamy expression had come over Marion's face. 'That's quite a good picture of my daughter,' she said, nodding in the direction of the wall above my head, 'taken two months before she died.'

I stood up to get a better look.

'No one would have called her pretty,' said Marion, 'not in the conventional way, but she has a very strong face, don't you think, full of character? Of course it was Wesley who found her and I sometimes think that was what she'd planned. Do you think that could be right?'

She wanted me to say something, but I knew so little about the suicide. 'Did she take an overdose?' I asked. 'Was it here, in the house?'

She frowned. 'Oh, I thought you knew. I thought Stephen would have told you. It was in the old sports pavilion, up by the playing fields. It's kept locked of course but Tricia had a key, so she could do her little cleaning job.'

'She cleaned the pavilion?'

'Yes, that's right. It's an unusual building, with quite a high ceiling. There's a room where they have meetings, or prepare the teas for after the cricket matches. She was hanging from one of the beams.'

251

Chapter Fourteen

Livvy's book of poems was in my filing cabinet. I took it out, flicked through the pages, and a sheet of paper fell out. Another poem? It was handwritten in large, spidery letters and round the edge of the paper was a kind of frieze of pin men.

I sat down, started to read, and experienced an unpleasant sensation that started in my stomach and spread up to my chest. Then someone knocked on the door.

It was Dawn Rivers. She looked agitated rather than irate. Even so, my heart sank.

'Are you busy?' She stood in the doorway. She was wearing an outfit I had never seen before: a black and white checked jacket, plain black skirt, black patent leather shoes. 'I wondered if I could have a quick word,' she said. 'I checked with Heather and she told me there was no one with you at present.'

'Come in.' I still had the sheet of

paper in my hand. 'I've just been reading something a client gave me.' Then I broke off, noticing her expression. This was no social call. Why would it be? We were not on those kind of terms.

'Martin Wheeler's coming back next week,' she said. 'I expect you're all very relieved.'

What could I say? 'Look, I'm sorry things have been a bit difficult. I suppose people get used to working together and they're not very good at adapting to someone new.'

She pulled out a chair and sat down heavily. 'No, you don't have to pretend.'

After all the things I had said about her, now I was trying to find reasons to let her off the hook. If she was a client I would have kept quiet, waited for her to explain, but she wasn't a client and my stomach was still clenched in a hard knot after reading Livvy's poem. 'Just a series of misunderstandings,' I began, but she interrupted impatiently.

'No, it's nothing to do with working here. I was wrong to agree to fill in, not while I was... But I needed the money. You see, I did something incredibly stupid.' She paused, giving me an opportunity to

253

imagine all the dreadful things she might have done.

'I've been seeing someone—for about two years. He's married.'

'Is that all!' It was an instant reaction, but the wrong one.

'He told me his marriage was over,' she said fiercely, 'then the week before I started working here he moved back in with his wife.'

All of a sudden the tight rein she had kept herself on for the past few weeks gave way and tears started to seep out of the corners of her eyes.

'I wish you'd told me before,' I said feebly. 'If you'd told us when you first came here.'

How could she have done? Confided in total strangers, who had made it clear, pretty well from the start, that they didn't like her very much? 'No, of course you couldn't. Look, I'm really sorry.'

'It's not as though it was unexpected,' she said, pulling a couple of tissues out of the box on my desk. 'I knew it was going to happen, I was waiting, I knew he'd been lying.'

'Doesn't make it any better though, does it?'

She blew her nose. 'I've been offered a job in Ipswich but I'm not sure. It would mean starting all over again. If I stayed in Bristol he might change his mind.'

I should have let her talk but I couldn't resist the temptation to tell her what to do.

'Take the job,' I said. 'Get right away from him, don't even keep in touch by letter. Guys like that are bad news.'

She managed a weak smile. 'You sound as if you're talking from experience. Anyway.' She stood up. 'I wanted to explain before I left. I felt it was only fair.'

'No, don't go yet. Look, later on maybe we could go out for a drink or something.'

She nodded vaguely. She had said what she wanted to, now she was anxious to return to her room and repair her make-up before her next client arrived.

I picked up Livvy's poem. 'Listen, I'm really sorry, Dawn, I feel awful about the way we've treated you. When's your next client? Have you got time to have a look at this? I'd really like to know what you think.'

She took the sheet of paper and I could see from her face that she thought I was asking her help as a way of making up for the past few weeks. I watched closely as her eyes moved slowly down the page, then back to the top for a second read.

'This is from one of your clients?' she asked. 'He or she wrote it specially—for you?'

'God, no. At least, I hope not. It fell out of a book she lent me. She writes a lot of poetry, has it printed by one of those vanity publishers.'

Dawn read it through a third time, then turned the paper in all directions, inspecting the pin men in their odd contorted positions. 'If I were you,' she said slowly, 'I'd be rather concerned, very concerned in fact, and not just about the welfare of the client.'

Ros had fixed up to see me, by herself this time, not with Livvy. I hoped, for once, she was going to talk about her own problems, but as soon as she arrived she started on a long story about how the doctor had been round when Livvy was still in bed, talked to her for nearly half an hour, then offered her a prescription that she had turned down flat.

'What was it for?'

'Oh, I don't know.' Ros gave an exasperated sigh. 'Tranquillizers, anti-depressants? But Livvy doesn't believe in any form of medication, unless it's prescribed by a homeopath or a herbalist.'

'She's not your responsibility,' I said.

'No, I suppose you're right. You mean, I'm probably doing more harm than good, encouraging her to talk. She seems to have given up writing poetry for the time being, says she's going to learn to paint.'

'Might be a good idea,' I wanted to tell her about the violent, erotic verses that had slipped out of the book, but that would only have encouraged Ros to spend the whole of her time discussing Livvy. 'Look, let's forget about Livvy just for the moment, and you can tell me how *you've* been feeling.'

'Me?' She laughed nervously. 'I suppose Livvy thinks since Tom was a painter...' Then she noticed my expression. 'No, I'm not changing the subject, I did want to talk to you, it's just, if I don't tell you about Tom it won't make sense about me and Stephen.' She paused, trying to work out the best way to explain. 'Tom was quite a good artist, I think, but that wasn't enough. He wanted to break new ground,

257

be the greatest painter of the decade. When he found that wasn't going to happen I suppose he became disillusioned. Then he met up with Neil Hyatt.'

She looked at me enquiringly, but I decided not to tell her how Erica had mentioned the name.

'Hyatt was a failed painter too, but he had a knack of making money. He persuaded Tom to do a series of prints and, when they sold for quite large amounts, convinced him the two of them could become rich without any great effort on either of their parts.'

'Did Tom tell you all this?'

'Tom? Oh, he'd never have done that. I suppose the two of us never really hit it off, but he and Stephen were great chums—for a time. Anyway, it seemed Hyatt had been right. The prints sold in their thousands. You can see them all over the place, hanging in hotel bedrooms, restaurants, airports, you know the kind of thing. Skilful, but totally without any artistic merit.' She paused, glancing at me, then looking way. 'I'm quoting Tom, not giving you my own opinion. Of course, after eighteen months or so he couldn't take it anymore.'

'Tom couldn't.' So far I had learned no more than Erica had told me already.

'I don't know what happened exactly.' Ros picked up a pen on my desk, then gave a nervous laugh and put it down again. 'Perhaps it was when he turned fifty. No, it was before that. Some kind of life crisis, you know the kind of thing. I believe he claimed to have had a kind of Road to Damascus experience, but then he always tended to dramatize. Anyway, the upshot was he turned his back on the whole prints business and announced he was giving up the art world and becoming a Christian.'

'Surely one doesn't preclude the other.'

She gave me a fleeting smile. 'With Tom it did. Of course, he'd invested all the money, made sure he and Erica would be comfortably off for the rest of their lives. Everything he involved himself in had to be a hundred per cent. D'you know the type? Art, money-making, religion. Is it possible to become addicted to helping people, high on good works?'

She laughed, but without any amusement. 'Of course Erica found the change of heart rather hard to take. I think they'd been close, once, and now he was out

259

all hours of the day and night, involving himself in everyone else's problems and never even noticing what was going on in his own family.'

'Was there something going on?'

'Sorry? Oh, just the usual things, I suppose. Bringing up two children, running a home. Anyway, after a time she started getting all these symptoms.'

'Erica did?'

Ros nodded. 'I suppose it was to get Tom's attention, but if that was her aim it was a miserable failure. Headaches, stomach aches, dizzy spells, then she started drinking. If it had been anyone else, Tom would have bent over backward to understand, do what he could, but as far as I can make out he just kept telling her to pull herself together.'

'It's not always easy with someone close to you.'

She gave me a hard look, then busied herself, opening her bag, searching for something that didn't seem to be there, then closing it again with a snap and placing it on the floor between her feet. 'No, you're perfectly right, and he certainly did a lot of good in the parish. He was loved, there was no doubt about that, only

I used to worry about the children. James could take care of himself, I imagine, but Sally... Tom was fond of her, and I suppose in that sense she was the one who suffered least, but what's going to happen now?'

'How was Stephen involved in all this?' I asked, trying to steer her back to talking about herself.

'Oh, Tom and Stephen were inseparable. In fact you could say Tom was almost like an honorary curate, although obviously he couldn't actually take a service. I used to wonder why he didn't go the whole hog and get ordained, or at least he could have trained as a social worker, but that would have meant taking notice of other people's opinions, and, in any case, they probably wouldn't have taken him on, he'd have been too old.'

'Did something go wrong between Tom and Stephen?'

She frowned. 'Wrong in what way?'

'You said they were great friends—for a time.'

'Did I? Oh, I don't know what I meant. They used to argue a lot, but only about theological issues—and things like the changing role of the parish priest.'

'And you think this affected Stephen's decision to leave the Church?'

She jumped slightly. 'Oh, no. No, I'm sure it didn't. That was because of this book, and as far as I can remember he'd started writing it before he and Tom had even met.'

I wanted to ask if she thought it possible that Tom Luckham had deliberately allowed himself to go into a hypoglycaemic coma. Marion Young seemed to think he suffered from bouts of depression, but Ros had said nothing about it and the impression she was giving was of someone who felt he had found a worthwhile way of life.

She had turned away from me and was looking through the window, breathing fast. 'Oh, by the way.' Her voice shook a little and just for a moment I thought I could sense fear. 'Have you seen Stephen recently? How's he getting on? No, I'm sorry, it's nothing to do with me, just as long as he's all right. He must miss the parish. He was so involved with his parishioners, with the old people of course, but I always thought he was particularly good with the families. He told you, I expect, the reason we never had children.

They say there's a new technique they can use these days, even when the sperm are practically non-existent, but I don't imagine the success rate is very high.'

When I returned home my neighbour from the ground floor was watering her pinks. She asked after Owen, then started talking about the woman who had moved into one of the flats opposite.

'She works at the university, Anna. I wondered if Owen knew her.'

'What's her name?'

'Canning? Canford? She was telling us how she's written a book on genius, people who've written music or made scientific discoveries.'

'Really?' I wanted to go up to my flat, but it was some time since Pam and I had had a proper chat. 'What's her thesis? I mean, how does she think genius comes about?'

'That's just it, Anna, I didn't expect her to tell us very much. I mean, it's not as though I know anything about that kind of thing, but Janos was there and he seemed interested, and once she'd got going...' She tipped the last drops from her watering can. 'She thinks it's all a question of parents encouraging their children, giving them plenty of stimulation.'

'Well, I suppose that's right in the sense that someone would be unlikely to become a concert pianist if his or her parents had never been able to afford piano lessons.'

Pam thought about this. 'Yes, but would the same thing apply if you gave a boy a microscope or a chemistry set?'

'Who knows?' The woman opposite sounded woolly-minded, but perhaps it was unreasonable to write her off on the basis of Pam's understanding of her work.

My phone had started ringing. I leapt up the steps, two at a time, wrenched open the door, and got there just as the answering machine had started its stilted, slightly embarrassing message. It was Stephen Bryce.

'It's about Clare,' he said. 'She's received some kind of anonymous letter and she seems to be working herself up into a bit of a state. I'm going round there, I wondered if you would come too.'

'What does it say, this letter?'

'She wouldn't tell me. She was crying, so was the baby. It all sounded a bit fraught. I know it's a bit much to ask, but I thought if we both went round. The letter—it could be something to do with Tom.'

It was starting to get dark. I stood on the pavement, watching the dipped headlights of each approaching car, trying to guess if it was Stephen's. While I waited I tried to work out the real reason Ros had been to see me again. To talk about her and Stephen, that was what she had said, but, apart from a brief reference to their childlessness, everything she said had been about Tom Luckham. When she asked if I had seen Stephen, the question had been followed at once by an insistence that I respect his privacy. Even so, she had probably noticed enough in my expression to convince her that Stephen and I had been in touch with each other. Had I imagined her anxiety? Was she worried in case Stephen had told me something that she would prefer me not to know? Perhaps she felt she had given too much away the time she had angrily described Tom as 'a failed artist'.

In the end Stephen's car came from the opposite direction I had been expecting.

'Took a wrong turning,' he said, pulling up sharply and winding down the window. 'Thought I'd found a short cut, then got confused by all the one-way streets.' He opened the passenger door and waited impatiently while I fastened the seat belt. 'Sorry to force you out like this, only if the police are going to be involved I feel Clare may need some guidance.'

'You told her to call the police?'

He shook his head. 'No, I told her to do nothing, not until we'd had a chance to discuss what had happened. The letter was waiting for her when she returned from work. It came through the post, a Bristol postmark, and the actual message seems to have been made up from letters cut from glossy magazines.'

'Where does Clare work?' I asked.

'In a factory that makes crackers and party novelties. Not really a factory, most of the work seems to be done by hand.'

'I thought you said she worked in a shop.'

'She used to.' He slammed on the brakes, just in time to miss a black and white dog meandering across the road. 'Up to last Christmas. Then she fell out with her employer. I forget exactly what happened. She was unemployed for a time, but she's a pretty determined girl. Around the end of January she found this new job, seems to enjoy it, mainly for the company, I expect—and the money of course.'

It took less than ten minutes to reach the hostel. Clare was up in her room. So were Wesley and Marion Young. Stephen started to introduce me to Marion, then stopped, probably wondering if we had met already, and if so, whether Wesley knew about it.

'Anna McColl,' I said, holding out my hand.

Marion took it in a firm grasp. 'I believe you've met my husband.'

Clare was sitting on a floor cushion, with her knees pulled up under her chin, and Wesley, who had let us into the room, was holding the offending letter. He handed it to Stephen and I read it upside down.

It was brief and to the point. 'ANY MORE LIES AND I'LL SHUT YOUR MOUTH FOREVER'. The letters looked as if they had been cut out by a child who had only just learned how to use a pair of scissors. The paste had spread out and dried in greyish blobs.

'Some nut case,' said Clare, calmly picking bits of dust off her skin-tight shorts.

Stephen had told me she was in a

267

terrible state, but if anything, she looked slightly bored. 'Anyway, I feel sorry for the poor cow,' she muttered. 'S'pose she thought I wouldn't dare tell anyone, just sit here shivering in me shoes.'

The rest of us exchanged glances.

'You must tell us who you think it was,' said Marion, lifting the baby out of his cot. She glanced at Stephen, wanting him to back her up, and he nodded slowly, then folded his arms.

Clare gave a kind of snort. 'When I opened it I got a right shock, I can tell you. Even thought whoever sent it might be on their way round. Then, when I'd calmed down, I realized that was crazy. I mean, if she don't want me to know who she is she's not likely to come here, is she?'

Wesley had been standing with his back to the rest of us, looking through the window. When he turned round I noticed how tired he looked. The bright-eyed expression I had noticed, when I called round at the shop, had disappeared. I wondered if he found his wife's interest in Clare a little difficult to take. Did he see it as a way of putting off coming to terms with Tricia's death? Perhaps it made him angry. How could someone like Clare ever make up for the loss of their only child?

'It would be a mistake to jump to conclusions,' he said, raising a hand to smooth back his soft white hair. 'You think you know who sent it, Clare, but you could be mistaken.'

Clare laughed. 'Anyone want a cup of tea then, or I could make instant, but I've only enough milk for Cain's breakfast so you'd have to have it black.'

No one took up the offer.

'It came in the second post, did it?' asked Marion, gently opening the baby's clenched fist to release a handful of her hair.

'Search me.' Clare scratched her thigh. 'First one doesn't get here till nearly nine.'

'And it was in an envelope with a stamp? Where is the envelope?'

'Tore it up, didn't I?'

'So, it'll be in the bin.' Marion refused to be put off. 'Was the address handwritten?'

'No, it was like in the letter, bits cut out and stuck.' Clare threw back her head. 'No, hang on, big black capitals with one of those waterproof pens. Anyway, I took the rubbish down to the big bins in the yard, not going through all that muck, and I told you about the postmark. Bristol it was and the envelope was white, nothing fancy, not scented or nothing.'

'That wasn't very sensible, throwing it away,' said Marion. 'It's part of the evidence.'

Suddenly Clare looked defeated. 'I told you, I'm not giving it to the police. When I phoned you Cain had been yelling his head off...that's why I'd got myself going. Now I can see the whole thing ain't worth bothering about.'

'I expect it was just a silly joke,' said Marion soothingly. 'Of course, if you get any more you'll have to report it, isn't that right, Dr McColl?'

Clare glared at me. 'Stephen shouldn't have told you. If you go to the cops I'll bloody kill you.'

'Don't be so stupid,' said Stephen. 'If they hear you've been receiving threatening letters they'll—'

'No!' Clare's shout was so loud that the baby let out a whimper, then started to cry. 'I thought you were my friends. I wish I'd never told you. As for her.' She jabbed a finger in my direction. 'All her type do

270

is stir up trouble, just so they can make more work for themselves.'

She frowned, then gave me a little smile, as if she regretted her attack.

'Listen, Clare,' I said, 'it's possible someone else knows you told us about the passenger in Tom's car.'

'What?' Her mouth trembled. She took Cain from Marion's arms and held him against her.

'What is it that makes you think the letter came from a woman?' I asked.

'I didn't.'

'I thought you said your first reaction had been to worry in case *she* called round.'

Clare hesitated, her eyes darting round the room, glancing at each of us in turn. 'Anyway, it's stupid,' she muttered, 'and whoever it was, they needn't have had anything to do with what happened to Tom.'

On the way back to the flat I asked Stephen if he thought Clare had 'written' the letter herself.

'The thought did cross my mind,' he said, 'but what would be the point?'

'To try to incriminate Erica? She seemed

adamant a woman had sent it and all along she's been telling me if I want to know what happened to Tom I should start with Erica.'

We were passing the Suspension Bridge. It was not the most direct way back to the flat, but letting Stephen choose the route was easier than giving him a string of directions.

'You shouldn't judge her too harshly, just because of her rather eccentric appearance,' he said.

For a moment I thought he was talking about Erica, then I realized he meant Clare. 'Nothing particularly eccentric about it,' I said irritably, 'practically a uniform among her age group.'

'Yes, I suppose you're right.' Stephen kept his eyes glued on the car in front. 'Anyway, you're in good company. Ros couldn't stand her, said she was the type that made fools of men, wound them round her little finger. Still, if you've talked to Ros you'll be aware of her opinion of men.'

When I said nothing he accelerated sharply, then suddenly pulled up next to the kerb and sat with his head resting on the steering wheel. 'I don't know if you're still seeing her,' he said, 'but if you are she'll have told you what she thinks of me. No practical common sense, head filled with useless ideas.' He sat up straight but kept his head turned away. 'I've been reading this book. Thinking, feeling, and sensation, the three aspects of us, all of which need to be developed and used in their proper contexts. Ros used to try and explain but I couldn't, or wouldn't understand.'

'What did Ros try and explain?' I was tired, wanted to get back to the flat.

Stephen turned towards me and there were tears in his eyes. 'Oh God. Oh God,' he kept repeating. 'Have you ever done something you regretted, then it was too late, there was no going back?'

'What kind of thing?' But he was too distraught to answer, just drove off without looking in the mirror, ignoring the angry hoot of the motorist coming up behind him.

Chapter Fifteen

If Clare had pasted on the letters herself did that mean she had made up the story about the passenger in Tom Luckham's car? But what was it all for? To make sure she was the centre of attention? When she first had the baby everyone had rallied round, doing everything they could to help, but now Cain was nearly a year old, things were changing. Marion Young still looked after him occasionally, but she had made it clear she thought it time Clare stood on her own two feet. Stephen called round at the hostel every so often, but since Ros's last visit I had given up any idea that he might be Cain's father. Of course, men with very low sperm counts had been known to father children, and imagine what Ros would have felt if she and Stephen had tried for a baby for years and years, then he had made another woman pregnant.

I was in my office, waiting for Lloyd to arrive. When his head came round the door he looked more subdued than usual and his words came out in a kind of low growl. 'You forgotten I was coming?'

'No.'

'I'm late.'

'Yes, but only five minutes. It must be a record.'

There was no smile and when he sat down he kept his knees pressed together, instead of sprawling his long legs across the floor.

'You married?' he said suddenly. 'Or ain't I allowed to ask?'

'No, I'm not married.' It was the first time he had asked me anything personal.

'Divorced?'

'No.'

He gave a heavy sigh, then looked up at the ceiling and sighed again.

'How's your chest?' I asked, sensing that he was going to force me to drag out whatever was bothering him, question by question.

'That all you're interested in?'

'No.'

'If you knew someone was cheating on someone, only the person it was happening to never knew, would you tell them or would that make it worse?'

'I'm not sure. It would depend.'

He yawned, but it wasn't a real yawn, just a way of relieving the tension. 'Thought it might be a one-off,' he said at last, 'only it ain't, she's been seeing him two or three times a week.'

'Who is it you're talking about, Lloyd?'

He looked at me as if he thought I was slow-witted. 'Me Mum, of course, and the bloke three doors down. What should I do then, tell me Dad or keep me mouth shut and let 'em get on with it?'

His arms were folded and he was staring at me defiantly. He wanted a straight answer, something black and white.

'How long have you known about it? Does anyone else know? Your brother?'

'Him? He's only a kid.'

'It might be best to talk to your mother first, tell her what you suspect.'

'Oh, it's true all right. Don't want me to go into details, do you, only I've seen 'em at it—well, good as.'

'Yes, I see.' This was a tricky one, but at least we could be getting to the real reason for his nervous habit. 'Is there a relative, or close friend of the family, you could talk to?'

'What good would that do? There's me

Mum's sister, in Kingswood. You mean she could speak to her.'

'It might make things easier for you.'

'Could give it a try, I s'pose. Reckon she'd give her hell.' His face broke into a nervous grin and he stuffed his hands into the pockets of his baggy trousers. 'Sorry about the tape but I thought it'd give you a clue, reckoned you were bound to guess who'd sent it.'

'Tape? It was you—'

'Listen to it, did you? Third track's the best.' He had stopped grinning and was eyeing me anxiously. 'Probably never even played it, just chucked it away.'

'No, I played it,' I said. 'Look, I wish you'd told me about your mother before. Still, it can't have been easy, I can understand why it took you time to come out with it.'

'Nah, stupid, should've told you the first time I come. That's it then, is it? I never knew what the hell to do so I started scratching off me skin while I was thinking about it, and all that stuff I told you about my brother and school and that... Must think I've been wasting your time.'

'How long have you known about your mother?'

He moved his lips, silently calculating the length of time. 'Since Easter, maybe before. Course, if me chest gets bad again.'

'Come back next week,' I said, 'and let me know what's happened.'

'Think I should?' He stood up and took a small packet out of his jacket. 'This one's better, more professional. Play it when you get home. Who knows, you might even enjoy it.'

I had seen Erica drunk before, but not like this. She was lying on a sofa with one of her feet on the floor and the other on the armrest. Her skirt had ridden up, revealing a large amount of fat, wobbly thigh, and her mouth was open so wide I could have counted her fillings. Sally sat close by, moving her head in time with her mother's snores and not bothering to wipe away her tears.

'I made her some coffee,' she said, 'but she spilt it on the carpet.' She pointed to a wet patch near the sofa. 'Is she going to die? A girl in my class said if you drank too much you could choke on your own sick. That's what nearly happened to her brother.'

It was two o'clock. Sally had let me

into the house, then hurried back to the drawing room where I found her attempting to rouse Erica, although it was clearly a lost cause. The cocktail cabinet had been left open and an empty bottle of brandy lay on its side on the coffee table. A large tumbler was wedged between Erica's foot and a pile of glossy magazines, some with their pages torn out and screwed up into balls.

'Don't worry,' I said, 'she'll be all right, she just needs to sleep it off. Come on, we'll go and sit somewhere else.'

Sally hesitated. 'Shouldn't we call the doctor?'

'No, I don't think that'll be necessary. This can't be the first time she's been like this, is it?'

Sally shook her head slowly, then walked towards the door, glancing anxiously over her shoulder at the figure on the sofa, then raising her shoulders and letting them drop in a gesture of resignation. 'Abigail says alcohol destroys your liver. Her mother was caught drink-driving but that was different, she'd been to a party.'

I had never been in the dining room before. It was dark and gloomy, with brown and cream striped wallpaper, brown velvet curtains, still partially drawn across, and heavy oak furniture. A round table, surrounded by six carved chairs, had been polished quite recently—I could smell the scented wax—but I had a feeling no meals had been served in the room for months.

'We used to have our supper in here,' said Sally 'when Daddy was...'

'Sit down then.' I pulled out two of the chairs. 'Is James upstairs?'

The tears started again. She moved her head but was unable to speak, and when I put my arm round her the sobbing increased. Eventually, between gasps she managed to tell me James had not been back for three days.

'Oh, well, I expect he'll be home soon. He often stays away for a night or two, doesn't he?'

She stood up again and pulled open a drawer in the sideboard, taking out a paper napkin, with sprigs of holly round the edge, and blowing her nose. 'Not for this long. I wanted the police to look for him but Mummy says he's too old.'

'What about the cleaner?' I asked. 'If your mother was feeling unwell couldn't she have helped?'

'She doesn't come any more. She and

James had an argument. I think she said something about Mummy. He told her she wouldn't be needed again. And Col's gone too.'

'The gardener?'

'He was nice, he helped when one of the guinea pigs escaped. He was making a new run but he didn't have time to finish it.' She covered her face with her hands and when she spoke again I had to struggle to hear what she was saying.

'I'm sorry. It was lies. Some of the things I told you.'

'What things?'

'I don't know. I got so muddled. The map in the car. I just said I saw it so you'd think I was trying to remember. James said... It's because of Daddy. James knows who did it.'

'Did what, Sally?'

Her face was swollen with crying and she had the paper napkin pressed to her mouth. 'Buzz thinks so too. They're going to get him—the person who killed Daddy.'

'Who's Buzz?'

'James's friend. I don't think his real name's Buzz. It's Brian or something.'

'Is James with him now? Where does he live, this Buzz?'

'I don't know!' She was shouting so much Erica must surely wake from her drunken stupor. But I could hear no sounds from the other room.

'Do you know who James thinks was responsible for your father's death?'

'No.' She was shaking, but less agitated. 'James didn't want me to talk to you. He thought I'd made a mistake.' She pushed the sodden paper napkin in the pocket of her shorts, then took another from the drawer.

'A mistake? What about?'

'About the person who tried to pull me into the car. Then he decided it mightn't be such a bad thing, you coming here, not if you could make the police find out what happened to Daddy.'

'James told you what to say to me? Listen, Sally, if you know...'

'I don't, I got it all wrong.' She drew back the curtains and began struggling to undo the window catch. 'It's so stuffy in here. I feel sick. You won't tell the police. If they find out...'

I tried again. 'Sally if you know who was driving the car...'

'I don't. I did. At first I did, but it wasn't right, it couldn't have been.'

Suddenly, she let out a squeal of delight. 'Oh look, it's Abigail.'

I joined her at the window. 'Your friend from school?'

'Can I let her in?' She was licking her fingers, rubbing her cheeks in a useless attempt to disguise the fact that she had been crying.

'Yes, of course, but you'll have to finish what you were telling me. Maybe Abigail can wait in your bedroom.'

'No, there isn't any more. I promise there isn't.'

'Who did you *think* it was, Sally, the person who...' But she was halfway through the door and a moment later I heard her greeting her friend with small excited cries.

I closed the dining room door and stood in the hall, working out what to do next. If James had real proof that his father's death had not been an accident, he should have gone to the police and told them everything he knew. But none of the people who thought Tom Luckham had been murdered seemed to have any actual evidence, apart from Clare Kilpatrick and it was likely she had made up the story about the passenger in Luckham's car.

Sally and Abigail stood in the doorway. Abigail was slightly shorter than Sally, but looked older. Maybe it was the designer jeans and jacket, and the way her hair had been cut in a short, fashionable style.

'I just called round to see if Sally was all right,' she said, looking a little shifty, as if she thought she should have come sooner.

'Yes, of course. I'm sure she's very glad to see you.'

Was it the first time Abigail had been to the house, and if so why had she chosen to turn up now? Odd sounds were coming from the drawing room. Sally looked frantic. 'I should take Abigail up to your room,' I said. 'I expect your mother would like a cup of tea. No, it's all right, I'll make it.'

Erica had woken up but was still slumped on the sofa. She narrowed her eyes, trying to make out who I was, then belched loudly. 'Is that you, darling?'

'It's me,' I said. 'Anna. Would you like some tea?'

'Tea,' she repeated. 'What time is it? I must have dropped off for a moment, didn't sleep very well last night, had a bit of a headache. Is James back?'

'No, not yet.'

'Where is he, d'you know? Oh, it's you, the psychologist.'

'I don't expect there's anything to worry about,' I said, although nothing could have been further from the truth. 'Have you any idea where he stays when he's not here? I remember you saying he sometimes crashed out with a friend.'

She sat up, rubbing her eyes. 'Sally's here, but they won't serve her at the off-licence. If you see James tell him to get some money out of the cash machine.'

'Sally's friend Abigail has come to see her.'

'Who?'

'A girl called Abigail,' I repeated. 'She's in Sally's class at school.'

Erica yawned hugely, then covered her mouth with both hands and spoke through her splayed fingers. 'Oh, the child with a mother who works for the BBC. Tom promised Livvy Pope he'd send her some of her poems for that programme that used to go out in the afternoon. Livvy's poems on the radio, what a hoot.' She hoisted herself up and sat with her legs stuck out in front of her. 'Poor old Livvy, I'm afraid her idol had feet of clay. You know, I don't think I'll bother with tea.' She reached for the empty glass that was lying on the floor. 'But if you could be a dear and top this up.'

Chapter Sixteen

I should have contacted Howard Fry straightaway, but I had clients to see and an appointment with Fay Somers, who had asked to visit the Psychology Service. In any case, Howard had shown little interest in Tom Luckham's death and whatever James knew, or thought he knew, was unlikely to contribute anything to the search for Geena Robson.

Fay was in the office, talking to Heather. They seemed to be getting on well and Heather reacted almost as if my arrival had spoiled the fun.

'Trouble?' said Fay, studying my face, then glancing at Heather. 'If I've come at an awkward time...'

'No, nothing that can't wait.'

'Sure?'

'Quite sure.'

Heather came close and lowered her voice to tell me how Dawn had given her a little present. 'Look, it's for the bath.' She held out a bottle of pale

287

green liquid. 'Wasn't it kind? Perhaps we misjudged her.'

'Yes, I think you may be right. Look, Mr Rogers is coming at four-thirty, isn't he?'

Heather checked the appointments book. 'Yes, that's right. D'you want me to give him a ring? If you're not feeling too good...'

'No, I'm fine, but if he wouldn't mind changing his appointment, coming in a couple of days' time. He lives quite close by and he seems to be free most days. Anyway, see what you can do.'

I took Fay up to my office.

'I just thought it'd be interesting to get an idea of how you all worked,' she said, casting an appreciative eye round the room. 'Something I can tell them back home. It's fascinating the way clinical psychology's developed in different parts of the world. In some ways we live in a global village, where research from all over becomes common knowledge, but in terms of applied techniques, well I guess different cultures have different ways of doing things.'

I pulled out a chair but she continued to stand. 'I've caught you at a bad time,' she said. 'No, I can tell.'

'Not at all. Have a seat. Well, let's think, there's three of us who work in this part of the city. Used to be four and, with any luck, we should be getting someone else in a month or two.'

'And your clients are referred by local doctors.'

'Not just doctors. Social services, ed. psychs, the child and family unit.'

'You see kids too?'

'Only the older ones.'

She nodded. 'Teenagers, sounds great. Treat them like adults, establish a relation-ship where they feel they've got your respect and the battle's already half won.'

It was no good, I couldn't give her my full attention. 'Listen, I'm sorry Fay, but since you're here d'you mind if I ask you something?'

'Fire away.' She folded her hands in her lap. 'I could tell you had a lot on your mind.'

'That evening at your flat. Jill phoned me not long after—to talk about Clare Kilpatrick, the girl with a child at the day nursery.'

'Really? She asked for your number but I thought maybe she needed some advice, something about one of the kids.'

'The thing is,' I said, wondering what it was about Fay that always made me want to confide in her, 'Clare's never told anyone the name of her baby's father. Well, not as far as I know. Jill seemed to be implying that she knew who it was, or thought she did, and if it turned out to be important she would be prepared to tell me the father's identity.'

'And is it important?' Fay was unable to hide her curiosity. 'I was round at the nursery one time when Clare was collecting the little boy. Got the impression she's quite a tough cookie. Her friend was there too.'

'Really?'

'Such a good-looking pair, but terribly young, and perhaps just a little irresponsible. I kind of assumed he was the baby's father. Luckham, yes I'm sure that's the name Jill mentioned. Or have I got it all wrong? Jill's a wonderful person but some of her mothers, I've a feeling they take advantage of her, expecting her to stay on longer after the place should be closed up. Well, I mean, you can't just walk away if a kid's waiting to be collected.'

'No, of course not.' I was wondering how much Jill had told Fay. If Jill's marriage was on the rocks and she was finding her job hard-going, she was probably glad to have another woman around the place. I could imagine her feeling sorry when Fay returned to Australia.

'This boy you saw Clare with,' I said. 'About eighteen, good-looking, thick fair hair, drives an old Ford Capri?'

Fay smiled, remembering. 'Don't know about the car, Anna, but I recognize the description. Nice-looking boy, looks a little like that kid that used to be in our most notorious soap opera, the one that's shown on your television twice a day.'

'The thing is, he hasn't been home for a couple of days. I don't think it's all that unusual but his sister's worried and there's some questions I need to ask him.'

'I saw him last Monday if that's any help.' She frowned, closing her eyes and scanning a mental map. 'I'd driven down Whiteladies Road, then straight on, past the big store, only I got in the wrong lane, you know how it is, and found myself in a queue of cars waiting alongside those fascinating little shops.'

'And you saw James? Was Clare with him?'

'No, he was with another lad, taller,

291

older I'd say, with his hair tied back in a ponytail. The lights were red, that's how I came to spot James, not that we've ever been formally introduced, but Jill's pointed him out a couple of times, says he's sweet with the baby, even collected him from the nursery one time when Clare was late back from work.'

'And you're sure it was James you saw?'

'Certain. The lights turned green but the traffic took a time to move off. I remember glancing over my shoulder and spotting the two of them disappearing through a doorway.'

'What kind of a doorway?'

She sighed. 'I'm sorry, Anna, I haven't a clue. Isn't there a shop that sells second-hand violins? No, hang on, it could've been a place that hires out fancy dress costumes. Well, it looked like fancy dress.'

I stood up. 'Look, I'm terribly sorry, but I need to clear this up straightaway. Can we meet up some other time, soon, for a meal maybe?'

'Need any help?' she said hopefully, springing up and taking her jacket from the hook on the back of the door. 'Oh, well, never mind, you've got my number, if there's anything, absolutely anything I can do. You know me, I'd be more than willing.'

The multi-storey car park was almost full. I managed to find a space on the top floor, then ran down six flights of stone steps, holding my breath to block out the stench of urine and stale cigarette smoke. A brief lull in the traffic left just enough time to dart across the road and, once on the other side, it was only a matter of seconds before I was standing outside the row of shops. It was a long shot—James had probably been visiting a friend, the man that Fay had seen him with—but it was just possible he had been staying there for the last couple of days.

There was no sign of the shop Fay had described, then I realized she must have meant the one that sold masks and comic wigs. The window was full of the kind of stuff young kids find hysterically funny: bleeding fingers, enormous blackened teeth, coils of plastic dog shit. Through a half-open door to the right I could see a yard with a couple of bikes leaning against the wall, and beyond that three or four tubs of orange geraniums.

When I tried to step inside the door stuck against the stone floor and I had to give it a hard push. At the same moment I thought I heard a sash window being pushed up, but when the noise of traffic faded there were no more sounds. A door to my left had a yale lock. Another had a latch, but when I opened it as carefully and quietly as I could it turned out to be a large cupboard, piled high with cardboard boxes. If I asked in the shop someone might know who lived on the first and second floors, if anyone did. The display of geraniums made it unlikely that the whole building was used for storage and when I stared up at a high window I thought I detected a slight movement, although it could have been the fleeting effect of a cloud passing over the sun.

In a useless attempt to drag open the door to the street without making a sound I succeeded in scraping the skin off the side of my hand. Blood welled up and, intent on finding something to staunch the flow, I failed to notice that a door at the back of the yard had opened.

'Looking for someone?' The accent was Scottish and less than friendly. I spun round and saw a tall man, with his hair tied back in a ponytail, watching me suspiciously.

'A friend,' I said.

'Name?'

'Sorry? Oh, the name of my friend? James Luckham.'

The man's eyes shifted towards the door on his right. 'And you're...?'

'Look, it doesn't matter. I'm a friend of his sister's, she's worried about him, I only came here on the off-chance.'

The man had circled round and was standing between me and the door to the street. It was only open a crack. I could see the passing traffic, an elderly couple standing by the zebra crossing, waiting for the lights to change, a woman carrying a red shopping bag.

The man had an amused smile on his face. 'You're the shrink, am I right?'

'I need to talk to James.'

'What about?'

We stared at each other. 'Just answer me one thing,' I said. 'You're Buzz, at least I assume that's who you are. Sally's afraid James is going to do something stupid. He's told her he knows who killed their father and he's going to—'

'Really?' He seemed to find this funny,

then his expression hardened. 'Tom Luckham was a bastard, but that didn't give anyone the right to snuff him out. You've been to Secker Gorge? Nothing particularly dangerous about it. You'd have to be drunk or sleepwalking to fall off those rocks.'

'D'you know a girl called Clare Kilpatrick?' I asked. 'Has James mentioned her name?'

'He might have.'

'Is he with her now? Are she and James...'

He started to laugh. 'You thought James was screwing Clare? It's not as if he's ever made a secret of his *"sexual orientation"*. Anyway, how did you know where to find us? Oh, I get it, you put the thumb screws on Sally.'

He was leaning against the wall, and now that I could study him properly I could see he was quite a lot older than James, probably in his late twenties or early thirties. It was an attraction of opposites: James with his thick, straw-coloured hair and blue eyes, Buzz with eyes that were almost black, and hair to match. James, however hard he tried, still looked as if he came from a privileged background, whereas Buzz had the appearance of someone who has had to fight every inch of the way.

'I have to go now,' he said. 'I've no idea when, or if, James'll be back so there's no point in you hanging around.'

I followed him into the street. 'You know who it is, the person James suspects of killing his father?'

'I'd have thought you'd have found that out for yourself by now. Providing everyone with a bit of psychotherapy is a novel way of investigating their darkest thoughts, I'll give you that, but how d'you know if people are telling you the truth? Even psychoanalysts must get lied to.' He ran a finger across the palm of his hand, as if he was measuring his life line. 'The female of the species,' he said slowly, 'isn't that what they say? Always deadlier than the male.'

For a moment I thought he was talking about me, then I realized it was more likely he was referring to the person responsible for Tom Luckham's death. Before I could ask what he meant he had answered the question himself. I had to strain to hear what he was saying, above the noise of an ambulance.

*'One gives, the other takes, but let me give.
You died, you had to die, so I could live.'*

The first poem in the book Livvy had shown me at Miller's Cottage. 'James has a copy of Livvy's poems?'

Buzz laughed. 'Hasn't everyone? Look, if you want to know more you'll have to talk to him yourself. If it wasn't for Sally he'd have left home long ago. He crashes out here when things get too heavy. Have you any idea what it's like spending half your time searching the house for bottles? She even had one hanging out of the bathroom window on a piece of string.'

'Please.' I had one last try. 'If you've any idea where I might find James.'

'Try the hostel.'

'Where Clare Kilpatrick lives?' But already he was halfway across the street, dodging between the double stream of traffic. When he reached the other side he paused, raising his hand in a brief wave, but without bothering to turn round. A moment later he had disappeared down the road that leads through to the Entertainment Centre.

Wesley Young was working in the front garden. For someone who claimed to know

298

nothing about flowers, he had produced a pretty impressive display, even though they were mostly the standard petunias and busy Lizzies that can be bought in bulk from any garden centre.

'Hallo.' I walked across to join him. 'Not in the shop today?'

'Half-day closing.'

'Yes, of course.' I had forgotten how some of the shops, away from the city centre, still closed on Thursday afternoons. 'I'm looking for James Luckham. You haven't seen him?'

He yawned. 'You've only just missed him. Called round to see if Clare needed any help. She was off sick yesterday with a migraine, still feels a bit groggy.'

'He's with Clare now?'

He yawned again, shaking his head, and my frustration started to get the better of me.

'You don't know where he went?'

'Afraid not. Important is it? Not his mother, I hope.'

There was no time to ask what he meant. Was Erica's drinking common knowledge? 'No, nothing like that, so you've no idea where he's likely to be?'

As I was leaving Wesley called me back.

'Only an idea, but he could've gone to Secker Gorge.'

'Why would he do that.'

He took a tissue from his trouser pocket and wiped his nose. 'Think I must be allergic to the pollen. He goes to the gorge quite often, hopes it'll help him work out what happened to his father that day. Can't leave it alone, but who can blame him. Anyway, I expect he'll call round here later on. Give him a message if I see him, shall I? Tell him you wanted a word.'

Chapter Seventeen

Secker Gorge. It was a long shot but at the very least I would see for myself the place where Tom Luckham's body had been found. Not the exact place—I had no idea where that had been—but the steep, rocky gorge that Howard had described, a place I had passed several times, but never actually stopped off to explore. There was nothing dangerous about it, that's what Buzz had said. Tom Luckham was a bastard but his death was inexplicable.

It was just after six. I crossed the Suspension Bridge, turned left down Rownham Hill, then under the flyover, following the signs to Taunton, the airport and the A38. I was thinking about Livvy. She was depressed, angry, hysterical, but was she capable of murder? Snatches of the poem, with the pin men frieze, came back into my head. *Suck the blood, warm and soft, between the lips, in hungry sips. Falling, hard, a seeping wound, thrusting in, a loving sin.* They were hardly memorable lines, but I had remembered them, rehearsing them in my head, wondering if the sheet of paper in the bound volume was Livvy's way of confessing, a sick woman who wanted someone to take responsibility for what she had done. Did James know something about Livvy and if so why had he kept it to himself since January?

I passed a church, some obscure denomination, with this month's improving message pasted on a board—CARPENTER FROM NAZARETH NEEDS JOINERS —and wondered what a theologian like Stephen Bryce would have made of it. Then I wondered if he had spoken the truth about his reason for resigning from his parish. Ros had never hinted that there had been anything else, apart from Stephen's loss of faith, but was it just possible something had happened that he had managed to keep from her? Or something they both knew about but wanted to keep from me? Something connected with Tom Luckham?

It was Stephen who had started me off, thinking Luckham had not died from natural causes. As far as Stephen was concerned, however urgent the phone call to the house had been, Tom would still have looked after his health meticulously.

According to Buzz, he and James were aware of my interest in the 'accident'. Motive and opportunity. All along I had been assuming the person who stole my bag and used my video membership card was the same woman who had tried to pull Sally into her car, but there were other explanations. I had been wrong about the sender of the cassette, and the theft of the bag could have been simply a random event, unconnected with anything else that had been going on. Or had someone been trying to warn me off, someone who feared that my interest in the Luckham family would lead to a new investigation into what had happened at Secker Gorge? Any number of people might have had the opportunity to kill Tom Luckham, but who was it who had the motive?

I passed a large comprehensive, closed for the summer holidays, and it reminded me how Sally must have walked home from her private school, the day the attempted abduction took place, aware that when she reached home she was likely to find her mother slumped in a chair, or still in bed. Women with a drink problem elicited very little compassion, whereas tranquillizer addicts—and in my opinion the problem of weaning someone off sedatives had been wildly exaggerated—were the subject of sympathetic articles and television programmes by the score. It was true that pills had to be obtained on a prescription—and were therefore seen as 'medicine'—but in other ways was there really that much difference? I wondered if Erica's doctor knew about the state she was in. Had all his attention been focused on her husband's diabetes, with Erica being written off as a neurotic, attention-seeking female?

Driving automatically, with only half my brain watching the route, I almost missed the turning off the A38. In front of me a slow-moving cattle truck had pulled into the hedge to allow a bus to pass. Even after it moved on I had to endure a frustrating fifteen minutes before I could turn right towards the Chew Valley lakes and the Mendips.

The air was very warm and still, and winding down the windows made little difference. My brain was buzzing with half-remembered snatches of conversation. Fay Somers describing how James had gone with Clare to collect Cain from the nursery. Sally, with a paper napkin pressed against her mouth. *They're going to get the person who killed Daddy.* But often it was the things people failed to mention that were the most important. Remarks that had seemed significant could have been intended to divert my attention away from the truth.

A small red car was following about a hundred yards behind. It kept the same distance and when I slowed down it slowed down too. All of a sudden it was overtaken by a learner driver on a motor cycle, who roared up behind me, then swerved out at a dangerously high speed and shot away into the distance. I turned a corner, pulled up on the grass verge, and waited for the red Peugeot, but there was no sign of it: either it had stopped or the driver had pulled into the Forestry Commission car park.

On my right a boggy area, covered in tall reeds, gave way to higher ground, rough moorland, broken up by low stone walls, many of which had gaps that no one had bothered to repair. A short distance ahead a flock of sheep had started squeezing through an open gate, pushing against each other so that one or two appeared to have been lifted off their feet. I slowed down to a crawl and a moment later a farmer on a tractor turned into the road, with his dog seated beside him, moving its head in all directions, watching as a second, younger dog rounded up the sheep. Another couple of miles and I would have reached my destination. Secker Gorge, a small, steep valley that had been created when pressures from inside the earth had moved great masses of rock, and a strip of something much harder than the surrounding limestone, had formed an impermeable floor so that a stream ran over the surface, rather than sinking through. Geology was one of Howard's interests, along with old churches and country houses, and he seemed to know the place quite well. During the past few weeks, any mention of Tom Luckham's death had been easily brushed aside in favour of a description of how archaeologists had found tools in the gorge belonging to Neolithic Man, and how the remains of bears and wolves had been identified.

Tom Luckham's car had been left in one of the lay-bys, designed as a passing place. Maybe he had thought few cars were likely to come along the single track road in mid-January, and as it turned out, if his car had not been spotted, it was likely he could have lain at the bottom of the gorge for days, or even weeks.

Parking my car well off the road, I started walking back towards the path that led down through the trees. In January the whole place would have looked quite different. The elms and oaks would have shed their leaves and the steep track might well have been wet with mud. Just now it was bone dry and very slippery. Every so often I lost my footing and had to grab hold of a branch or a thick fern. I was descending fast but I could see the high rocks on the opposite side, although it was impossible to tell where the path led up to the top. Everything, apart from the ferns, looked parched.

I thought about Livvy and her crazy poems. Was it guilt, remorse, that had caused her to cut her arm with a razor blade? Was something in her crying out to be punished, but if that was the case, why not just admit what she had done? My brain conjured up an image of her phoning Tom Luckham early in the morning, persuading him to accompany her to the gorge, then confessing her love for him and expecting it to be reciprocated. How would he have reacted? With kindness, sensitivity, or would he have told her not to be such a silly little fool?

The path had flattened out, then, almost immediately, it started to climb. There was a short cut, but only a fool would have tried to use it. A broad band of small, loose stones, like an enormous children's slide, stretched from where I was standing right up to the rocks at the topmost point, but there was nothing to hold on to, no ferns or tree roots, whereas the path ahead of me was narrow, and winding, but had trees and bushes on either side.

No one was about, but Howard had said the place was often deserted. Tourists were more interested in visiting Cheddar Gorge or Wookey Hole. Secker had no giftshops or cafés, just a network of paths, some of them partially overgrown, and a steep climb for anyone prepared to make it, that looked as if it would provide a fairly spectacular view from the top. I was concentrating on keeping a foothold, but the thoughts that had been going round in my mind kept returning. Descriptions of Tom Luckham that made him out to be some kind of superman had always had the effect of making me think he was too good to be true. When Marion Young suggested he suffered from bouts of depression, I had jumped at the idea as an alternative explanation for what seemed to be a compulsive wish to help other people. Filling every moment of his day was an escape, but every so often the depression overwhelmed him. He had talked about it to Tricia Young. Why? Because they were both diabetic? But the girl had still been at school and was surely not the best person to understand the anguished soul-searching of a middle-aged man, who felt he had failed as an artist.

The rocks that marked the top of the gorge were now in sight. I was out of breath and my feet had started to hurt. Tricia Young. There was something about the suicide of someone so young that produced feelings of anger and regret, even in people who barely knew the victim. Surely something could have been done to stop it. However bad the person had felt, was there no one who could convince her that in a week, a month, things would look different? Three A's at A level, but she had only managed two B's and a C. *Only two B's and a C.* It was a perfectly good result but not in her terms.

I had reached the top. As I rounded a couple of bushes I took an involuntary step backwards. There was no real danger, not where I was standing, but if I moved any further forward I would be very near the edge. Below me was the stony slide, and from high up it looked even steeper. In the distance I could see Wells Cathedral, and beyond that the unmistakable outline of Glastonbury Tor. Shading my eyes against the evening sun, I turned to see if it was possible to spot the coastline, Clevedon, or Weston, and it was then that I heard the first sounds. Someone was crunching up the path. At first I thought I had imagined it, but when I listened carefully there was no doubt they were human footsteps. What of it? I was visiting the place. Why not somebody else? Maybe there were people who came here regularly, to watch birds or study the plants. There could even be people employed to make sure the paths were safe, or to cut back some of the undergrowth.

He came out into the open and I felt my throat constrict. In spite of it being such a warm evening he was wearing a dark jacket and thick grey trousers. He had a heavy stick in one hand.

'You were expecting me,' he said. 'You saw my car.'

An image flashed through my mind. Pam with her watering can. The woman who had moved into the house across the road. An expert in 'genius', who believed high achievement was simply the result of having encouraging parents. *Encouraging parents.* It was one of those moments when you realize that what feels like a revelation is really something that has been going round in your brain for days. I had allowed myself to be persuaded that Livvy Pope was the killer. I should have used my own judgement, thought things out properly. Now it was too late.

'You were in the red Peugeot?' I said, my voice sounding thin but surprisingly steady.

'The van's off the road. Bloke I do business with lent me one of his.' He was breathing hard, his chest rising and falling beneath his brown checked shirt. 'Tricia loved it here. The first time we brought her she couldn't have been more than seven or eight. Of course we never came up this far, not until she was older.

You need proper shoes.' He glanced at mine. 'Those aren't strong enough.'

'You told me James might have come here.'

He gave a sad little smile. His white, silky hair was moving up and down, lifted by the breeze at the top of the gorge. 'Marion did what she could to warn you—the bag, the video, explaining about Clare—but still you kept asking questions, stirring up trouble. Stephen knows nothing. He only kept in touch with you in the hope you'd persuade Ros to go back to him.'

'It was Marion who stole my bag?'

'She thought there might be notes, files, something that would tell her what was going on in your head, then when she couldn't find anything—'

'She used my video card. When she asked me round to the house it was because she wanted to find out how much I knew. What did you mean "explain about Clare"?' I was playing for time, keeping my eyes focused on Wesley, but also searching for a way to escape.

'Clare told you she'd seen me in Tom's car.'

'No, no that's not right. She thought it

was a woman, a woman wearing a head scarf.'

He didn't believe me. 'That's what she told Stephen, but when she was talking to you... I could see from your face...you knew Marion had sent that letter.'

'To Clare?' The more he said the better. Keep him talking, try to establish a relationship, but didn't we have some kind of relationship already? To someone in Wesley's state of mind anything that had taken place between us before would be irrelevant. Then I remembered how Wesley himself had dropped the first hint about Livvy. *That Pope woman thought he* (Tom Luckham) *could walk on water.* The slide projector. He had used it to lure me to the shop...

'Clare knew,' he said. 'She told you the letter had come from a woman.'

'I thought she meant Erica.'

'Erica.' He stared at me as if he thought I was mad. 'For Marion's sake. I did it for Marion. Why should he go on living when Tricia was dead? And the others. All the others. He used people to make himself feel important, to inherit the kingdom of heaven.'

'So you brought him here,' I said. It was

313

a statement, not a question. 'And pushed him over the edge.'

He smiled to himself, then the smile vanished and was replaced by an angry clenching of the jaw. 'I phoned from a call box and said Marion had gone missing. You see, his being Tom I knew he'd come straightaway. It was still dark, too early for his insulin but he brought everything he needed, and his breakfast of course in a special container like a kid's lunch box. We drove round for a bit, then I suggested Marion might have gone to the gorge, the place Tricia loved best.'

'But really she was still at home.'

'She'd have made a lovely nurse,' he said softly. 'What's wrong with being a nurse? Oh, but Tom could never leave well alone. *You can do better than that, Tricia, you could be a doctor, I know you could.*'

It was very quiet. If I shouted it was just possible I would be heard by someone in the farm I could see in the distance. Just possible, but not at all likely, and what effect would it have on Wesley?

'He wasn't dead when I left him,' he said. 'Someone might have found him before it was too late.'

'He'd broken both legs.'

His face was expressionless. 'You see, I only wanted to talk, make him admit what he'd done, but he wouldn't listen.' His eyes left my face for a second, as he looked at the steep drop, but I was too frozen to the spot to move. 'God's will, that's what he kept on saying. You must try to see it as God's will. He even wanted us to pray!'

He was small, but he looked strong. On the other hand, he was much older than I was. If I made a sudden movement, darted past him and started running down the path would he be able to catch up? First I would ask a few questions, try to get him off guard.

'You realized Clare had seen you in Tom Luckham's car?'

'I don't care about myself,' he said softly, 'but I couldn't leave Marion all alone.'

I edged a little closer to him. 'Tom had given himself his insulin but—'

'Tricia was a diabetic. Exertion uses up carbohydrates, causing a drop in blood sugar.'

'What happened to Tom's breakfast? You made sure he never had a chance to eat it.' My voice sounded unnaturally calm. It was as if I was listening to somebody else talking. 'If his car was found in a lay-by how did you get back to Bristol that day?'

'Walked to the Wells Road, then hitched a lift. Told the bloke in the car my van had broken down farther back. A German bloke, he was, on holiday, travelling round the West Country.' Suddenly he grabbed hold of my wrist and pulled me closer. 'That's the reason she waved him down, noticed the registration, knew he'd probably be gone before anyone got round to asking about hitchhikers.' His face was screwed up in pain. 'Forgive us our trespasses as we forgive those that trespass against us. Vengeance is mine saith the Lord but I say unto you...' Suddenly he broke off, realizing his mistake.

'*She* waved him down,' I repeated. 'It wasn't you who came here with Tom. Marion told him *you* were missing.'

His face was very close to mind. His eyes were brown with hazel flecks. 'Tom's daughter was still alive,' he said. 'He and Erica still had a daughter.'

'It was Marion who tried to pull Sally into her car? Look, I can help you, I know I can. Marion wasn't thinking straight. Her grief, the pain of losing Tricia.' But he wasn't interested in anything I might have to say. He had relaxed the pressure on my wrist, but when I moved slightly it tightened again.

'I'm sorry,' he said, staring at the drop below us, 'but I have to think of Marion.' Sweat was pouring down his face. He was pulling me backwards, we were very close to the edge, and the rock under my feet felt as slippery as ice. I glanced up at the sky, hoping to make Wesley do the same. Then it happened. He let go of my wrist and the sudden freedom made me lose my balance. With arms flailing, I tried to force myself to defy gravity. It was no good. I was suspended in space, like a diver on a high board, but there was no water below me, just shale and rocks. The sheer drop must have been less than ten feet but it jarred my whole body and as soon as I landed I started to slide. Further down a group of rocks jutted out of the scree. If they stopped me from falling any further..but I had no control over where I slid...and I was gaining speed all the time. Instinctively I tried to shield my head, flinging out a leg in a useless attempt to alter the position of my body, feeling the impact as my shoulder made contact with one of the rocks. My head jerked to one side. I heard a voice calling my name...from a long way away...then everything went black.

Chapter Eighteen

He was kneeling beside me. We were halfway down the slope, near the part where the stones gave way to rough grass and scrubby bushes. He must have edged his way across to where I was lying. It couldn't have been easy.

'Where does it hurt?' His voice was different, softer. 'Anna? It's me. Wesley's gone.'

I struggled to open my eyes wider. 'James?'

'No, don't say anything. Look, I'll have to call an ambulance, but first we'd better—'

'No, don't go.' I managed to haul myself onto one elbow. 'My arm, it's only my arm. How can we get down to the bottom?'

He looked doubtful. 'You may be injured more badly than you think.'

'No, I can tell. If you crawled across, that means we can both crawl back. Where's Wesley?'

He shrugged. 'Who knows? He never saw me. Look, it's not so steep here, you go first and I'll make sure you don't fall.'

The pain in my arm was getting worse but there was nothing much wrong with the rest of me, apart from a searing headache and the feeling that all my exposed skin had been rubbed raw. Very slowly I started moving towards the grass, searching for places where the stones flattened out a little, dragging myself a few feet, then tensing, waiting for my body to start sliding all over again.

James was slightly below me and making good progress. He had hold of my good arm and with his free hand he was reaching out to grab hold of some exposed tree roots. 'It's all right, we're nearly there, just a few more yards.'

My head was thudding. Everything looked blurred. Clutching at the grass, I could feel it slipping through my hand, then James pulling me clear of the stones, and dragging me onto the grass. 'Try and sit up,' he said. 'Lean against me, you'll feel better when you can see where we are.'

We were still fairly high up. There was no path, but the grassy slope was in ridges and there were plenty of bushes to hang on to. I looked back the way we had come, then up at the rocks at the top.

'How you feeling?' James was wiping the sweat off his face.

'All right, I'm all right, but how did you know...' Then the bile rose in my throat and I swung my head to one side and threw up on the grass.

We were on our way back to Bristol. My arm had stiffened up, my whole body ached from head to foot and I couldn't stop shivering, but somehow we had managed to get back to the road. Anything was better than being left there, alone. My head still ached, but the muzziness had been replaced by an odd feeling of euphoria.

'But how did you know where I was?' I asked.

James was driving too fast. He changed down to overtake an ancient blue van. 'Jude, at the hostel, overheard Wesley telling someone answering your description I'd probably gone to the gorge. Look, are you sure you're OK, only it'll be another half hour before we reach casualty.'

'You saw me with Wesley?'

He nodded. 'Then I watched you fall. I was certain somebody had gone with him that day—Clare had seen someone in the car—but I thought it was Livvy. She was crazy about Dad, right from when he first started going to Stephen's church. Then when he found a publisher for her poems.'

'Yes, I know, I read one of them. It scared me stiff.'

'Really?' He turned his head, wondering perhaps if I was suffering from concussion. 'How stupid could Livvy get, but I suppose if it made her happy. Then, one day, she heard him laughing.' He turned his head to make sure I understood the enormity of what had happened. 'He'd invited a few people back to the house, old friends from the days before he "saw the light". Livvy'd called round to see Mum, then she left and Dad started doing one of his famous Dylan Thomas impersonations. It was crazy, he was like two people. The great philanthropist, puffed up with his own importance, but when he saw his artist friends he could just slip back into how he used to be. Livvy came back to the house she'd forgotten her scarf or something, and overheard the whole thing.'

'He was reciting one of her poems?'

'What a bastard. Livvy wasn't the only

one who'd like to have hit back at him, but try explaining something like that to the cops. And it was so much easier to call his death an accident, and wrap up the whole thing with the minimum of effort and paperwork.'

I was thinking about Livvy. She had found out what Tom was really like but it still hadn't broken her attachment to him. After he died she had been able to wipe the unpleasant memory out of her head, and idealize him even more. Or had she? Then I thought about Wesley. Had he really believed a second death at the gorge would be seen as another unfortunate accident? But I doubted if he had worked things out that clearly.

James had gone silent. I asked if he had known Clare a long time.

'Clare? No, only since Dad died. I had this idea he could have been Cain's father, but it wasn't right although Clare let the woman who runs the nursery think Dad was responsible.'

'You're sure?'

'Oh, she'd have told me. Clare's OK, but she can't keep anything a secret for long. She doesn't know who the father is. A one-night stand, some college student?

Sometimes she studies Cain's face, and tries to see a likeness, but it's best not to know, that way you can avoid all the hassle at the benefit office.'

'Stephen seems fond of the baby,' I said.

'Stephen Bryce?' He laughed. 'You know Clare, loves being the centre of attention. I guess that's why a lot of girls have babies. First Dad, then Stephen and Marion Young. Listen, you're sure it was Wesley who killed Dad?'

'Not Wesley,' I said, 'it was Marion.'

'Marion?'

'He wanted me to think he was responsible, but he let slip the fact that it had been Marion who hitched a lift back to Bristol that day. I think her real intention was to force your father to face up to why Tricia committed suicide. I visited her once but she gave me an entirely false impression of how she felt.'

'Wasn't that exactly what she intended?'

'Yes, of course. She wanted me to think your father had committed suicide, and she kept going on about how Clare should be left to stand on her own two feet.'

'She didn't want you to guess who had been the passenger in Dad's car. It was

Dad who encouraged Tricia to train as a doctor. He should've gone into politics, that way he'd really have been able to control other people's lives. What d'you suppose Wesley and Marion will do now? Make a run for it, or give themselves up to the cops?'

'Who knows?' I was wondering if Marion had actually pushed Tom Luckham or if, like me, he had simply lost his footing. Was Tom really responsible for Tricia's suicide, or had Wesley and Marion gone along with the plan for a place at medical school, then blamed Tom as a way of coming to terms with their own guilt and remorse?

We were passing a field with six or seven horses, two of them foals. One of them was on its side and I remembered how, as a small child, I had seen a horse lying down and burst into tears, thinking it was dead.

'I think it was Marion who tried to pull Sally into the car,' I said.

'What! Did Sally tell you that?'

'No, she was confused, afraid of making a mistake, making people even more impatient with her.'

'She doesn't really know Marion and

Wesley. I suppose she must have seen Marion in church, but she doesn't go any more, not since Dad died. God, I should have listened to her. To be honest I thought she might have made up the whole abduction thing, then I kind of half-persuaded her it could have been Livvy.'

'So she made up how she remembered the "abductor's" perfume.'

He shrugged. 'Livvy always drenches herself in the stuff. I guess she's some kind of hygiene freak.'

The windscreen was misting up. He turned up the heater and switched on the fan. 'It was because of Dad that Mum started boozing,' he said. 'After he died I thought... Oh, I don't know what I thought, but it was too late by then, she was hooked. I hated him, thought she was well shot of him, but I guess she didn't see it that way. She was miserable when he was alive but after he'd gone, if anything she was worse.'

The countryside had given way to a new housing development, a children's playground, an estate agent and a shop selling flowerpots and garden gnomes. If the traffic was not too heavy we would be at the hospital in ten to fifteen minutes. I started to thank James for following Wesley's van, but he interrupted to say it was more out of curiosity than because he thought I was in any real danger.

'That time on the Downs,' I said, 'when you drove up close behind me...'

'I wanted to make sure you came back. Guessed you were the kind of person who reacts strongly to having pressure put on them.'

'You know, for a time I thought you and Clare...'

'Then Buzz put you straight.' He drew in a deep breath, then let it out in a long, despairing sigh. 'Look, I know this isn't the best time to ask, but is there anything you can do for my mother?'

'I thought you'd be in bed,' said Chris. 'If I'd known they were going to let you out I wouldn't have bothered.' She opened the box of chocolates she had given me and started studying the selection. 'Strawberry Creme. Fudge Delight. Anyway, I can drive you home and you can tell me all about it.'

I opened my mouth to explain, then saw Fay Somers coming through the swing doors at the end of the ward. She was carrying a huge bunch of flowers, wrapped in cellophane. How long had everyone expected me to stay in hospital? A couple of nights, just for a broken arm, had seemed excessive, but the nurse had said they wanted to make sure there was no concussion.

Chris looked up, saw Fay approaching, dressed in a long, floral skirt, and white skinny-rib top, and muttered: 'Who the fuck is that?'

'Fay,' I said loudly, taking the flowers and holding them to my nose. 'You are kind.'

'How are you?' She looked genuinely concerned. 'This is all my fault. If I hadn't told you I'd seen James Luckham.'

'I'm really glad you did.' I introduced Chris and she gave Fay one of her gushing smiles.

'So you're feeling better?' said Fay. 'When I heard what had happened... Jill told me. James had spoken to Clare and—'

'Who's Clare?' said Chris.

'Just a girl with a baby. I'll tell you about it later.'

She sighed. 'All right, I know when I'm not wanted.'

'Oh, don't be so silly.' But both she and Fay looked as if they were about to leave.

Howard Fry was standing just inside the swing doors, staring at my bed. He raised a hand but stayed where he was.

'Friend of yours?' said Fay, jerking her head in the direction of the swing doors. 'Look, can I give you a ring in a day or two? I'd love for us to get together before I go home.'

'Yes, of course, make sure you do, or I will.'

Chris bent to give me a kiss. 'Come on,' she muttered, 'I'm not going till you tell me who he is. It's your policeman, isn't it? God, why didn't you tell me he looked so stunningly forbidding?'

Chapter Nineteen

We had left the city and were heading north.

'The Cotswolds,' said Howard. 'We'll drive to one of the beauty spots, have a look round a few junk shops, then eat a large cream tea.'

'It'll be packed out with tourists.'

'So we'll have to wait our turn. Now, tell me about your vicar. He never really thought Tom Luckham had been murdered, just wanted you to persuade his wife to come back to him?'

'I doubt if it was quite that simple. The trouble is, people open up, confide in you and you start believing they've told you the whole truth. Stephen thought Ros wanted a divorce—because she was so angry he'd resigned from his job—and Ros thought, now he'd given up his parish, he had no more use for her.'

'Some marriage,' said Howard unsympathetically.

'Oh, come on, people often find it hard

to talk to each other. He once asked me if I'd ever done something I really regretted.'

'And have you?'

I ignored this. 'I think Stephen meant, at the time he left the Church, he should have made more effort to save his marriage. Or maybe he wished he'd never written his book.'

Howard pulled into a lay-by and reached for a road atlas lying on the back seat. 'Wesley Young's disappeared,' he said, 'and his wife. The house is empty and none of the neighbours has any idea where they've gone.'

'But you'll catch up with them,' I said, 'and then what will happen? If you want my opinion, Geena Robson going missing reawakened all Marion's suppressed feelings about her own daughter. Sally's attempted abduction was never a serious threat, just a way of frightening Erica. Her daughter was still alive, Marion's was dead.'

'All surmise, Anna, but no doubt you'll be able to persuade the jury the balance of Mrs Young's mind was disturbed. In any case, just for the present we're more interested in Geena Robson. She's been found.'

'Oh, no! Why didn't you tell me? Where was she?'

'No, don't look like that, she's alive.'

'Alive? You mean, she's all right? Who found her?'

He was turning the pages of the map. 'She phoned her mother. Apparently she'd been living in Lincoln with some man she met in the central library a couple of months before they ran off together.'

'But I thought she was seen climbing into a woman's car.'

'Yes, well we all make mistakes. Who's to tell, just by looking at the back of someone's head. Hippie type, with a ponytail and steel-framed glasses.'

'Why didn't she get in touch with her mother before?'

Howard shrugged. 'You never met the mother. To listen to her you'd have thought she and Geena were inseparable. Most parents become expert in deluding themselves, I suppose it's the only way they can survive.'

It was a cool breezy day, but inside the car it felt pleasantly warm. In the distance I could just make out the two bridges across the Severn Estuary and, on the other side, Newport and the grey strip of Welsh coast.

Howard stretched out a hand and touched my arm.

'Still hurting?'

I shook my head. 'James thought Livvy Pope had killed his father.'

'Who the hell's Livvy Pope?' His face was only inches away from mine. 'And if James Luckham knew something why didn't he come and tell us?'

I thought about Owen on the other side of the world and told myself today, this afternoon, didn't count. We were rounding things off, wrapping up a case, doing a bit of debriefing. Howard was watching me. He frowned, as if he had just remembered something. I started to explain about Livvy's poems, but I never finished what I was going to say. His arm was round my neck. I felt a sharp twinge of pain as the weight of his body crushed my injured arm against the tenderness of my aching ribs. I didn't care.

The publishers hope that this book has given you enjoyable reading. Large Print Books are especially designed to be as easy to see and hold as possible. If you wish a complete list of our books, please ask at your local library or write directly to: Magna Large Print Books, Long Preston, North Yorkshire, BD23 4ND, England.

This Large Print Book for the Partially
sighted, who cannot read normal print, is
published under the auspices of

THE ULVERSCROFT FOUNDATION

THE ULVERSCROFT FOUNDATION

. . . we hope that you have enjoyed this
Large Print Book. Please think for a
moment about those people who have
worse eyesight problems than you . . . and
are unable to even read or enjoy Large
Print, without great difficulty.

You can help them by sending a donation,
large or small to:

**The Ulverscroft Foundation,
1, The Green, Bradgate Road,
Anstey, Leicestershire, LE7 7FU,
England.**
or request a copy of our brochure for
more details.

The Foundation will use all your help to
assist those people who are handicapped
by various sight problems and need
special attention.

Thank you very much for your help.